After the Fall

Book 2 of the Roman Time Travel Series

Morgan O'Neill

C R I M S O N
R O M A N C E
Avon, Massachusetts

This edition published by
Crimson Romance
an imprint of F+W Media, Inc.
10151 Carver Road, Suite 200
Blue Ash, Ohio 45242

www.crimsonromance.com

ISBN 10: 1-4405-5151-0
ISBN 13: 978-1-4405-5151-2
eISBN 10: 1-4405-5131-6
eISBN 13: 978-1-4405-5131-4

Dedication

FOR MY FOUR "SISTERS," S, C, C & K, WHO'VE BEEN MY TRUEST AND MOST STEADFAST FRIENDS SINCE LONG BEFORE ANY OF US REALIZED GROWING UP COULD BE SUCH A CHALLENGE.

- CARY MORGAN FRATES

FOR MY MOTHER, WHO HAS BEEN WITH ME SINCE THE BEGINNING, IN LIFE— AND IN LOVING SUPPORT OF MY LITERARY ADVENTURES.

- DEBORAH O'NEILL CORDES

I was stunned and stupefied, so much so I could not think about anything else day and night . . . My voice sticks in my throat, and, as I dictate, sobs choke my utterance. Rome, the city, which had taken the world, was itself taken.

- Jerome, Scholar and Monk of Bethlehem, A.D. 410

PART ONE

Chapter 1

Autumn, A.D. 408, near Rome, Italy

The sailboat rode the chop up and down, steady in the face of chaos.

Salty mist bathed Gigi Perrin's face as she kept watch over the bow. The skies overhead were clear and fiercely blue, reminding her of Magnus's eyes. The wind and waves had just enough kick to make the afternoon perfect, and she sighed with contentment.

"Gigi! Gigi! Where are you?"

Gigi frowned. Her mother's voice was frantic. Hadn't Magnus let her parents know she was up on deck, manning the helm?

"Gigi! Where are you?"

Now her father? He sounded like he was crying! Gigi called out to them, but the wind carried her voice away. She tried to lock the wheel on autopilot, so she could go down below and reassure them everything was okay, but couldn't find the mechanism.

A hand clamped over her mouth and a jolt of fear went straight to her gut. She let go of the wheel, wrenched away, and faced her attacker. Honorius! The boat lurched sideways with the waves and Gigi fell, Honorius landing on top of her. She struggled, which made him laugh. She tried to knee him, but he was ready and caught her leg, pinning it to one side.

No! No!

He hit her on the jaw and the pain made her mind reel with terror. They were naked, and he was pushing at her, pushing . . .

"No!" Gigi screamed, thrashing at her cloak. Opening her eyes, breathing hard, she looked around. Rolling hills. A sea of dying grass gently waving in the breeze. The rough bark of a tree against her back. Emperor Honorius wasn't here. He hadn't touched her, hadn't been anywhere near her.

She wiped her mouth, then ran her hands over her face. Would she ever get him out of her nightmares? Would she ever be able to forgive herself for leaving her parents without a word? It hadn't been her fault, but . . .

She sighed and leaned her head back, a single tear trickling down her cheek.

Time travel. Sometimes Gigi had difficulty believing it had actually happened to her. She shivered despite the sun's warmth, wondering what it was going to be like spending a winter in ancient Italy. Living rough with the Visigoths, she'd be without all the things she'd taken for granted: central heating, modern medicine, chocolate.

But she was here. That was that. She looked at the beautiful hills again, seeking solace in the sight. Slanted sunshine, autumn's last gift, the air scented with grass and thyme. She held her hand out and her ring caught the light, the image of the goddess Victoria shimmering, dancing.

Magnus's ring, lost by him in battle, then found by her grandfather after 1,600 years, hers now, her wedding ring. Time travel had brought Gigi and Magnus together, the how of it unanswerable, the ring the key in some unfathomable way.

She touched her ring, recalling the past few months. Magnus. Always by her side, the only one sharing the secret of her other life. Their trek south through the rugged Apennines had been long and tiring, but they had persevered together. And now, finally, they were on the outskirts of Rome. What would happen next?

Getting up, Gigi brushed off her skirt and resettled her cloak. She looked at the jumble of buildings on the horizon. Rome. She was excited and nervous all at once, not only because she hoped to be reunited with her friend, Princess Placidia, but also because this was where the Visigoths would make a stand, perhaps the final stand against the Western Roman Empire. If all went well, they might just get land of their own, land they'd been promised by a string of emperors in return for decades of military service. More Romanized than the other so-called barbarian hordes, the Visigoths had fought with and eventually become part of the imperial legions, only to be spit upon and further abused by the Empire, until they supported open rebellion against its tyranny.

Gigi's mind returned to that coward, Honorius, and she was relieved he was far away, hiding behind the walls of Ravenna. Nevertheless, he still lurked in her nightmares, but she would fight him there, too, determined to put an end to her bad dreams forever.

Would she be able to succeed? Gigi took a deep breath and hoped so as she walked back to the Visigoth tents. She held her hands before a campfire, enjoying the play of warmth against her fingers, her ring softly glowing. Some women sat nearby, humming as they sewed and knitted. She greeted them, and they smiled back in welcome.

There was a sudden rise in conversation and Gigi turned just as a group of six men and one woman exited King Alaric's tent. With a gentle yet noble bearing, Queen Verica nodded to her husband and left to attend her own business. Gigi found it interesting Verica had equal standing among the men, something the Romans and their emperor disparaged as barbaric. Recalling how Honorius delighted in abusing women, Gigi knew without a shred of doubt the identity of the real barbarian.

She considered King Alaric and the other men standing by the tent. They looked serious and proud, especially the king and his second-in-command, Verica's brother, Athaulf. Gigi found confidence in their strength, and gratification in the way they'd offered their protection.

Her husband came out of the tent, an upstart Roman who had also thrown in his lot with the Visigoths. Quintus Pontius Flavus Magnus. His name reflected great heritage and high honors. Gigi felt a burst of pride when she recalled how he had bravely defended her after she was enslaved by Honorius, how he had engineered her escape. Then, with a death warrant on his own head, he had barely made it out of Ravenna. But they were now free!

She almost laughed as she envisioned him riding a white horse. Magnus had his back to her, bending an ear to Athaulf, who considered him an equal. He was valued here, and she could see how much he had changed, his confidence reborn, now that he was out of the emperor's evil shadow.

Sunshine lit her husband's dark brown hair, now almost long enough to start a braid in the Visigoth style. Gigi loved how he looked, loved even more all the little things he did to show how much he cared: making certain she got the first taste of whatever was served; letting her ride his horse, Agrippa, for hours as they traveled, and when she walked, placing himself between her and the jumble of wagons for safety's sake.

Gigi smiled, her will to succeed, to embrace this life, fully restored, and she marveled at how everything had changed since she'd met him. *Magnus, I adore you.*

Just then, he turned, searching the camp as if sensing her presence and the intensity of her thoughts. His gaze found hers, and he gave her a long look back. *Soon,* he told her, love lighting his blue eyes. *Very soon.*

She entered their tent and dropped onto the bed. Home. Not much considering what she'd had in her other life, but it was everything she needed here. She picked up her flute and idly played scales, wondering what Magnus would say if she could snap her fingers and show him what she used to have: her new digs in LA, and the charming, centuries-old family farmhouse she was having restored outside Avignon. Considering he was a Roman, she'd make sure he saw the big Jacuzzi tub in her LaLaLand abode, surrounded by vanilla candles, a bucket of champagne, and some luscious chocolate truffles.

Gigi laughed. That stuff might be necessary to enhance the mood with another guy, but she didn't need it with Magnus. He just had to show up in this tent and . . .

Magic happened.

She played a tune that had been running through her head, "That Old Black Magic."

The tent flap opened, and Magnus walked in. His face broke into a wide grin, and Gigi put down her flute. It didn't matter where she lived—he was her life.

"Oh, yeah, my Magnus," she smiled, "pure magic."

Chapter 2

Rome, Italy

Placidia stood on a balcony of the Domus Augustana, on the side of the palace overlooking the Circus Maximus. She breathed deeply of the crisp, fall air and caught a hint of the distant sea. Persia. India. Exotic places, so far away, yet were they truly beyond her brother's reach?

She had no answer. Honorius had the right, the duty, even, to use her marriage to shore up his alliances in this ever-changing world. But his choice of General Constantius did nothing in this regard. The general derived what power he had from Honorius, so her brother was treating her as nothing more than common booty, to be drooled over and played with, and, ultimately, caged like a dainty bird.

Constantius. Placidia cringed at the memory of his bulging eyes, balding pate, and thin smile. Fifty-odd years of fighting and court intrigue and military regimens. Set in his ways and much too old. God Almighty, she was only seventeen!

Would she be brave enough to seek her freedom when it came time to marry Constantius? Freedom. What did it actually mean? Slaves longed for it, of course, and debtors wanted to be free of their debts, but didn't everyone desire something other than what they had? She sighed, feeling guilty for worrying so selfishly about her own situation.

"Placidia?" Elpidia said, coming outside. "Priscus Attalus has arrived."

Placidia nodded to her old nurse and smoothed her gown, her thoughts in turmoil even as she strove for calm. What was happening in Ravenna? After Honorius murdered General Stilicho, two senators, Attalus and Magnus, had abandoned the city *and* her brother, each escaping a fate identical to Stilicho's, if the rumors were true.

And now her cousin Serena, Stilicho's detestable widow, had come to Rome. Ruined and impoverished, she had dragged along her surviving children, her young son, Eucherius, and her daughter, Thermantia, the emperor's discarded wife. Realistic about her own shortcomings, Placidia didn't know if she would extend a helping hand if Serena showed up on her doorstep, but shrugged it off. She admittedly felt the need for revenge, after all Serena had done, but the need was a burden unto itself, and Placidia wondered how long it would be before guilt overwhelmed her.

"Greetings, O most exalted Placidia," Attalus said.

"Welcome, O most excellent Attalus. Please take your ease. Have you any word from my brother? Or from Magnus?"

"There has been no word from Magnus, nor any hint of his whereabouts. It's as though he dropped out of Italia altogether."

She frowned. "No word at all? Not even rumors?"

"None. But fear not, dearest princess, for Magnus is Magnus. He will survive. As for the emperor, I received a letter from him this morning, which is why I sought an audience with you. Although it is addressed to me, I believe it is meant for your eyes as well."

Attalus handed over the rolled parchment, and Placidia quickly opened it and read:

"Priscus Attalus,

We were most decidedly vexed by your unanticipated leave-taking from Ravenna, but we understand your fear, for we have received word the Visigoths have left Noricum and are heading south."

"His royal 'we' annoys, does it not?" Placidia asked, then caught herself, remembering her manners. It would be unseemly to speak more about Honorius's conceit. She looked up at the senator. "Does this mean the Visigoths are on the march again?"

"Indeed, I'm afraid they will spread like a plague of locusts," Attalus said flatly. "But know this, I did not leave Ravenna with my tail between my legs because of the damnable Visigoths."

"I know." She swallowed. "But . . . do you know where they are heading?"

He shook his head. "I have heard they made plans to attack Ravenna by sea."

Placidia took a breath. Magnus had said that was a possibility. "Then the barbarians are fools. They will not succeed."

She resumed reading:

"As to the main point of our royal message—we care not if the Roman citizens hate Serena. There must be no housing in any royal properties and no bodyguards given her or any of her family. MAKE SURE OUR SISTER PROVIDES NONE! We would not want the boy to grow up weakened by overprotection. As to our former wife, let her EARN her bread.

With all esteem and sincerest regard,
Flavius Honorius Augustus, Emperor of Rome."

Placidia frowned and met Attalus's troubled gaze. Her brother had not changed, would never change, his selfish disregard for all but himself still paramount.

Knowing Rome seethed with hatred for Serena because of her loathsome deeds, Placidia said a swift, silent prayer for the two remaining innocents of the family. Thermantia and Eucherius were not responsible for their mother's desecration of pagan temples, her burning of sacred books, or her utter deceit. However, without bodyguards, their lives were as good as forfeit, for the mob would have its vengeance if they were ever recognized.

She crossed herself. "I must help them."

Attalus looked surprised by this, and so, she realized, was she. But then, Honorius had not thought of everything.

As to financial succor, he had said nothing at all.

*

The Avenue of Janus was hot, noisy, overcrowded, and stank of human sweat and garlic. Serena left the pawnbroker's shop and eyed the street carefully, mindful of the purse of coins hidden beneath her *palla*. The last of her jewelry had brought this final pittance, and she worried where she would get more money once it was gone.

Slipping back to the doorway of her tenement house, she was relieved to see Thermantia waiting there with Eucherius. They set off together without a word, and Serena breathed easier when no one caught her eye, nobody looked suspicious or seemed to care about their presence.

The crowds at the market had always terrified her. She didn't trust the plebian hordes, and knew they would attack if they discovered her identity. Unwilling to leave her children unprotected at the tenement, her only other choice was to bring them along when she did the shopping.

"Pull your *palla* close, Thermantia," she said in a harsh whisper. "I don't want the plebs recognizing you. Eucherius, keep your head down, and don't draw attention. Now, come."

They moved down the street as one. Suddenly, the hair on Serena's arms rose and she tensed, but there was no shoving, the sounds hadn't changed, the faces around them wore expressions of boredom.

All's well, just keep moving, Serena told herself.

They turned right, onto a better street lined with more prosperous shops, heading toward Quirinal Hill, to the Great Market. Serena saw Thermantia cast a longing glance at the window of an *unguentarius*, and she scowled at the girl—cosmetics were the last thing they could afford. She heard hawkers shouting from butcher and wine shops and smelled her favorite bakery's delicious fresh bread and *pulmentum*, the scent of the rich barley cakes making her stomach growl.

She had never experienced a time when she'd been so hungry, for so long. She glanced at her son and drew a deep breath. He looked thin and unhappy. She decided to visit the baker first, for the man was always happy when she flirted with him, and he let them sample his specialties before she bought anything. It was a good way to alleviate their hunger.

Serena quickened her step. "Hurry, keep up, children."

"Mother!"

"Hush, Thermantia," Serena scolded. "Your accent gives you away. Can't you remember a thing I—"

Serena saw the flash of sunlight on metal and instinctively threw up her arms, saw the arching, terrible swiftness with which the blade tore through the air, saw the edge embed itself and then slice across the neck of her beloved . . . her sweet babe . . . Eucherius!

Oh, dear God in Heaven! The murderer darted away, carrying something round and dripping in his hand. *No! Oh Lord, no! No!*

She started to run in the opposite direction, terrified she would be next, crashing through the people who stood and stared.

A wail rose up, a high-pitched keening. Serena halted in her tracks, listening to the horrible cries, then turned back, fearing the certainty of what she would see.

There, kneeling, Thermantia rocked, screaming and weeping, holding Eucherius's gaping, headless body against her own.

*

Thermantia watched as her mother lay curled on the floor of their squalid tenement.

"Oh, my dearest," Serena cried. "Please, hold me. I cannot bear any more grief."

It was the second day since her little brother's murder, and her mother had done nothing but bewail her misfortunes. Serena's eyes were puffy slits, her face blotchy and red, her hair undone and in a shambles. She was a disgrace to her family and dishonored Eucherius's memory by this endless display of self-pity. Where was the evidence of nobility to which she was born? Where was her pride?

Thermantia had stood alone, dignified, stoic, and brave when they'd buried her brother's headless corpse. Alone she had represented the family as her mother writhed on the floor at home, alone she had endured the pain of saying goodbye. And now her mother wanted comfort from her?

Enough is enough!

Serena checked her sobbing for an instant and looked up with a startled expression.

Did I say that aloud? Thermantia wondered.

"Sweet girl, please don't be angry," her mother sank back onto the floor and started in again. "Hold me. I have lost everything. Hold me, please."

In a fury, Thermantia crouched and grasped her mother by the hair, snatching her head off the floor.

Pitiful, disgusting, covered with snot and tears, Serena raised her arms, pleading, "Don't strike me, please, my dearest."

"You bitch, how dare you whine and wail and ask me for comfort!" Thermantia thundered. "You have done nothing but use us, use everyone you ever knew, for power, for prestige, for standing. You married off my dear sister Maria to Honorius, to be shamed and brutalized unto death, but that was not enough, oh no! Then you handed me over for the same, and the same he gave me. But I survived, because you could not wait to hand over one more, your own husband, and he was slaughtered! That makes two . . . two dead because of you. And now you have seen your son butchered before your cowardly eyes because of your words, your plotting, your plans, and then . . . you ran away! That makes three! Three within your own family whose blood is on your hands, yours and yours alone! May God curse you for the wretched human being you are!"

Her mother stared back at her, unmoving, silent for the first time in days.

Something in her mother's eyes, something deep inside her own mind, told Thermantia she had gone too far, much, much too far.

Don't say another word, she told herself. *Don't do this, don't give in to the hatred or . . . or you will become what she is, and you mustn't, no, you must never let that happen. You must never become like her!*

"I'm sorry, Mother," Thermantia whispered, releasing and smoothing her hair. "Forgive my harsh words, it was the grief speaking, only my grief."

Weeping, Thermantia knelt beside her mother and gathered her into her arms, cradling her, soothing her, rocking her. "We shall get through this together, Mother. Worry not. Shhhh, now, Mama. It will be all right, you'll see."

*

Placidia wrote the last few words on her waxen tablet, put the stylus down, and smiled at her steward. "That should do it, Leontius. Please see the funds are quietly gotten to poor Thermantia. She has endured much because of her mother's endless machinations, and now her brother's murder, and I shall do my utmost to see to her needs. Honorius would treat his former empress as a leper, but he has no feelings for anyone but himself, does he? Tell Thermantia the old royal villa at Capreae will be made available for her use, and arrange for an escort."

The steward nodded. "Your will be done, *Domina*—"

The door to Placidia's office crashed open, and Leontius sprang up to protect her, but the intruder was only Elpidia.

"My apologies," she began breathlessly, "but I heard noises and shouting in the street and went to see what was going on. Everyone is yelling that barbarians have descended upon Rome! Can it be true? Have you heard anything?"

Stunned, Placidia glanced at Leontius.

"*Domina*," he said, "I shall go to the Forum to see if the Diurnal has been posted with any news." He headed for the door, but found the way blocked by the sudden arrival of Senator Attalus.

"Forgive the intrusion, O most exalted Placidia," Attalus said, "but I must speak with you immediately."

Elpidia's hand went to her mouth. "It's the barbarians, isn't it? Dear Lord, it's not the Huns come all this way, is it?"

Attalus looked from Elpidia to Placidia, then shook his head. "It's the Visigoths, King Alaric and many thousands of his people, not just the warriors. They are within several *mille* of Rome—of all of Rome. The city will soon be completely surrounded, cut off. As to whether they plan to attack, or lay siege, or simply to parlay with us is as unclear as this tactic is unprecedented."

Placidia could feel her heart madly thumping. King Alaric and his people! Why had no one seen them coming? Where were Rome's scouts? Why hadn't the army stopped their advance? She knew the military was in total disarray because of what Honorius had done to General Stilicho. So many barbarian soldiers had deserted the ranks that the legions in Italia had been decimated. It was impossible to believe, but had the Empire decided to let Rome fend for herself?

She glanced down at her shaky hands, then clasped them together in an attempt to control herself. What should she do? Send to Honorius for help? Was there time? Would her brother even care? No, probably not.

Attalus cleared his throat. "Placidia, know this . . . the walls of Rome cannot be breached. We are safe here. And King Alaric is honorable, in his own way. I do not believe he will do anything unprovoked, or without warning. If it pleases you, I shall send out a delegation, or go myself, to find out what is on his mind and if there is anything we can do."

"How I wish Magnus were here to deal with this," Placidia said as she walked to the balcony to look out. "Where is he, Attalus? He knows this king and his ways. What does the Senate say about this?"

"Some are drinking, some pray, most are pissing themselves," Attalus replied. Leontius grumbled and Attalus smiled grimly. "Forgive my tactless words."

Placidia waved her hand. "Never mind. There is all too much truth in what you say. We've had little besides doddering, nervous old men occupying the Senate chamber these many years, and few, if any, were born with a spine."

"Until they receive word from the emperor, they will look to you for leadership and guidance."

Would they? Placidia wondered if this were true as she gazed out the window.

"Placidia, what say you? Shall I go to Alaric?"

She turned back to Attalus. "I believe you must. Find the king and bid him send emissaries to meet with me tomorrow eve, so we may sup together and speak in peace. Assure him it is no trap—upon my word—his ambassadors shall come and go without harm. And tell him . . . " Placidia paused, thinking. "Tell him I am willing to hear his grievances, for they must be serious indeed, if he is taking this action."

Attalus put a hand to his chest and bowed. "As you say, O most noble Placidia, so will it be done."

She watched him leave the room, then turned to her nurse and steward. "We will be having company tomorrow, if I'm not mistaken. Please see the banquet room in the House of Livia is prepared, Elpidia, for I think its coziness will not overwhelm our guests like any of our royal palaces would. And Leontius, I have heard the Visigoths like beer, so make certain there is plenty of it, along with meat, lots of roasted meat."

Chapter 3

Gigi and Magnus sat by the campfire with King Alaric. The sun was almost down, the full moon rising. She took a sip of her beer and yawned.

Magnus saw this and made a move to rise. "With your permission," he said to Alaric, "I believe it is time we retire to our tent—"

There was a sudden commotion, and a man raced forward, then dropped on one knee before Alaric. "My king," the man said, "a Roman emissary has arrived. He has requested an audience with you."

"Bring him here," Alaric said.

Magnus exchanged a look with Gigi. She glanced at his hands, so steady, no hint of nerves. She gripped her mug, striving to match his calm. Who was coming? What was going to happen now? She turned as several Visigoth scouts walked forward, escorting a lone, balding man with a fringe of graying hair, wearing a white toga bordered with purple.

"Attalus, you old dog," Magnus exclaimed, leaping to his feet.

"Magnus?" The man looked stunned. "Well, damn me straight to Hades! We were all wondering what had happened to you."

The two Romans clasped forearms, then embraced.

Attalus glanced at Gigi. "I see you found your beautiful flute player."

Magnus grinned. "Indeed. My Gigiperrin. And now she is my wife."

"My sincerest felicitations," Attalus said, slapping Magnus on the back before turning to Gigi. "It is about time someone tamed this grizzled warrior."

"It wasn't easy," Gigi laughed.

Alaric broke in, "Priscus Attalus, welcome. What brings you here?"

Attalus bowed. "O most excellent King Alaric," he intoned,

"I am here to extend an invitation on behalf of the *Nobilissima Puella,* Aelia Galla Placidia. She desires to meet tomorrow eve with ambassadors of your own choosing to discuss our mutual concerns. She plans a banquet in their honor and ensures their safety within the walls of Rome—and their safe return."

Hearing this, Gigi felt her heart race with anticipation. Magnus must have felt the same, because he quickly said, "King Alaric, if I might be so bold, sending Gigi and me would be seen as a gesture of friendship."

"I concur," Alaric agreed. "The two of you shall go to Rome, to sup with Galla Placidia. And Athaulf shall accompany you. He can speak for us and shall benefit from a look at the city, to see her full splendor, before . . . "

The king let his voice trail off, and Gigi saw Attalus pale ever so slightly, as if he understood, as if he knew what was coming.

*

The next day, Gigi, Magnus, Athaulf, and Senator Attalus and his bodyguards rode their horses along the Via Salaria toward Rome. As they drew closer, the city's massive walls and then the Salarian Gate came into view. It was a solid, rather plain archway of squared stones, with a gallery above flanked by two brick towers. They were manned by soldiers wearing the Roman-style, bristle-topped helmets. People streamed through the gate, while hundreds of wagons and carts congested the road.

"I never imagined it would be so crowded," she said to herself, wishing she could share this with her grandfather, her dear Grand-père, who had loved studying the ancient world, especially Rome.

Senator Attalus moved his horse alongside. "Within the walls, there are perhaps one million people. Far too many, if you ask me. We patricians are few; the rest are the *plebecula,* the masses who even now care for little else than bread and circuses." He shrugged. "And, because of the overcrowding, we must leave our horses here and proceed inside on foot. We shall have a contingent of imperial guards protecting us from the plebs."

Honorius's thugs? With a shiver, Gigi handed off her horse and strained to see beyond the gate, looking for big, hairy German-types with axes. She shot Magnus a glance, glad he was less recognizable these days, then adjusted her *palla*, attempting to hide her face.

Before they passed through the gate, the men stopped and urinated in urns provided by the guild of fullers, to facilitate the bleaching and dying of their cloth. Gigi turned her head away, embarrassed to watch a bunch of men peeing, and wondered where she might go. Magnus assured her public latrines were placed at regular and convenient intervals throughout the city.

They continued on, pushing their way through the throng, to where the *Palatini* guards stood waiting. Their leader saluted Attalus, then briefly eyed Magnus and Athaulf. Gigi hazarded a glance at the man, but there was nothing telling in his gaze, no hint of interest or recognition. The other soldiers stood at attention, carefully training their eyes on the distance. She felt a small measure of relief as the party set off, although her *palla* was still close about her face.

The chaos of the Roman streets was astounding compared to Ravenna, the noises every bit as loud as any modern metropolis, but the smells were different—a combination of wood smoke, fish, and garlic, loads of garlic.

Roma, Caput Mundi—the capital of the world. How different the city looked, how ancient and splendid. Gigi gawked at the throng, multiethnic and mostly young, all moving in a swirl of tunics and gowns. The Roman Empire's reach was vast, but she was still surprised to see the occasional person with jet-black hair and slanted eyes, clearly someone from central Asia or beyond; some were richly dressed merchants, but others wore simple tunics and had pierced ears, the mark of slaves coming from the Far East. The Empire's connections with the northern realms was evident, too, in that many of the younger Roman women had blue streaks in their hair, a new style copied from the barbarians of Britain.

Then Gigi spotted three women wearing togas and tugged on Magnus's sleeve. "Do you know them? Are they senators' wives?"

Magnus laughed. "No, women don't wear togas unless they're prostitutes. It is their way of flaunting Roman law, for only male citizens may legally wear the toga."

"So, you're saying you don't know them?" Gigi teased.

He winked at her and she went back to gawking. People haggled with shopkeepers or filled water jugs from fountains, while others begged for alms or ate where they stood. She even saw one couple having sex in broad daylight under the archway of a building.

Gigi grabbed Magnus's arm, but he was already watching. "In public?"

"Ah, perhaps she is but an impulsive lass, giving him a gift this day," he replied, laughing. "Here is my Rome, in all its grime and glory."

Their party moved on, past an area Gigi recognized—barely—as the Forum. It was stunning to view it whole, not in the tumbledown state she was used to seeing. Soon, the sun dipped behind a building, but up ahead the Coliseum still gleamed, its marbled walls catching the last rays of sunshine. Huge. Breathtaking.

Magnus nudged her and pointed. "That is the Palatine Hill, where we're headed, and on its summit is the great palace where Placidia resides."

More exquisite marble, columns, and balconies, pinked by sunset.

Gigi nodded and smiled. She was excited to see Placidia after so many months, and the prospect of spending a night in luxury with Magnus was tantalizing. She could hardly wait.

Chapter 4

The Visigoths would soon arrive!

Placidia stood in the Garden Room of the House of Livia, awaiting King Alaric's ambassadors. The last light of day filtered through a trio of lunette windows, illuminating the walls and their ancient frescos with a pearly glow. She loved this room with its lush depictions of Livia's country garden, the walls painted with garlands, fruit trees, and birds. It was one of the true glories of Rome, revered since the time of Livia and her husband, Emperor Augustus, and lovingly cared for by their successors.

Placidia could sense their presence still, and knew she must protect Rome as they had done. She had to find a way to convince the Visigoths, make them understand this great city should never be destroyed. She bowed her head, praying to God she would find the words to save her people, her world.

A tap at the door, and she nervously looked up as her nurse stepped into the room, holding a jewelry box.

"Ah, your gown is exquisite in this light! You look beautiful, dearest," Elpidia gushed. "That shade of green matches this emerald necklace perfectly."

"My favorite color."

"For good reason. Please turn around and I'll put it on you."

Smiling, Placidia touched her chignon, then gathered stray tendrils away from her neck and waited until Elpidia was done.

"There is still time to get bracelets and earrings, Placidia. I fear you look too plain with but one necklace. A princess of the Empire should glitter in gold and gems."

"This is quite enough. I am not here as a bauble on the emperor's arm." Placidia adjusted her necklace, gorgeously decorated with alternating emerald prisms and gold beads. She glanced in the mirror, moving her head ever so slightly until the image was clearer, and was pleased by her look. "Tonight, I am Rome. Elegant, powerful, worthy of honor."

"Glorious," Elpidia added. "You, my dear, should be empress and not—"

"Shush, those are treasonous words!" Placidia shuddered.

"*Domina?*" Leontius tapped on the door. "Your guests have arrived."

Placidia's heart thumped, and she glanced at Elpidia. "Show them in, Leontius."

He opened the door and Senator Attalus entered with a tall, bearded man, who bowed low before her, then raised his eyes to meet hers.

The barbarian was so handsome! Placidia could hardly breathe and labored to keep her expression calm and welcoming.

"O, most noble Placidia," she heard Attalus intoning, "may I introduce Athaulf, brother-in-law to King Alaric and second-in-command of the Visigoths."

Placidia stared. Athaulf's beautiful eyes were hazel with flecks of emerald-green, so radiant, so full of life and humor and, and . . . passion! Tremors, like little shock waves, tore through her body, leaving her flushed and weak. He looked as surprised as she, and his gaze bore into her, holding her fast, refusing to let go.

The room was silent, the air pulsating, waiting, and Placidia knew there was something she must say, but she couldn't find the words, couldn't even find her voice.

She opened her mouth to speak, blinked, and tried to swallow, but her throat was too dry, and still he held her, caressed her, reached into her very soul with his wondrous eyes.

"A-hem, O most gracious Placidia." Another man stepped forward and went down on one knee, as did the woman standing beside him.

Athaulf dropped his gaze and Placidia's wavered, then broke, and she drew a deep breath as she turned to the other two. They knelt before her, their gazes fixed on the floor. Flustered, she realized the man's voice had sounded familiar, and she stepped closer, trying to see his face.

"Please rise," Placidia said. "Do I know you?"

The pair got to their feet, the man towering over her.

He smiled through his heavy beard. "I believe you do, under less hairy circumstances."

Placidia gasped, then abandoned all decorum, launching herself into his arms. "Magnus! Magnus! Oh, how I have missed you!"

Magnus laughed, hugging her tenderly. "And I have missed you, dearest Placidia. Rome is treating you well, I hope?"

"Of course," she replied, wiping her sudden tears. "We have so much to talk about, so much catching up to do. Oh, Magnus, I am so glad to see you!"

His eyes twinkled mischievously. "There is someone I would like you to meet. May I present my wife?"

"What?" Stunned, Placidia looked at the woman beside Magnus, and as recognition dawned, they fell into each other's arms, laughing. "Gigi, dear, dear Gigi. I thought you dead, and knew Magnus's heart would surely die with you. What a blessing this is! What a blessing to see you both again, and married—for love! I knew it! I just knew how strongly you felt about each other!"

Behind her, Placidia heard Attalus clear his throat, and she reluctantly disengaged from her friends and returned to her duties, carefully avoiding the hazel eyes that had so captivated her moments before.

"Please forgive my, er, inattention," she said to Attalus. "I hadn't expected such wonderful gifts. I am in your debt, for you have restored my friends to me, but perhaps I can repay it in some small amount, by treating all of you to a banquet." She sensed Athaulf's eyes on her, but forced herself to concentrate on her responsibilities as a royal hostess. "For now, let us dine and enjoy each other's company, and when we have had our fill of good food and fine wine and beer," her eyes flickered unwittingly to the irresistible Visigoth, "we might be more easily disposed to discuss your king's concerns, and the reasons that bring you to Rome."

*

Placidia lay in her bed unable to sleep, her head roll clasped tightly to her chest. It was clear: Magnus and Gigi had turned their backs on the Empire forever. They would do everything in their power to protect the city of Rome and her people, and Placidia in particular, but the heavy demands of the Visigoths were not negotiable, and their allegiance was now to them.

Already, she had sent envoys north to Ravenna, to inform Honorius of King Alaric's demands, to inform him they now held Rome hostage, and to plead for payment, for his intervention in the situation, so the siege might be quickly lifted. It horrified her to be so closely linked to an emperor who had done so much harm to this landless people.

And then, there was the king's brother-in-law, Athaulf, and it was to him her mind constantly returned, refusing to stay away long, refusing to dwell on mere matters of state. She had never before felt the blood flowing hot and powerful in her veins, like it did every time she looked at him, every time their eyes met.

Placidia moaned and rolled over, unable to remain calm as she recalled his eyes, his smile, the shape of his lips against the goblet of wine.

How she wished everyone else had left the banquet! How she wished to taste those lips, to feel his hands upon her. She could still smell his scent, the heady fragrances of leather and lavender. And she remembered how his gaze had locked with hers again and again, how he looked as if he could devour her with his eyes, as if he too wished they were the only ones in the room.

She sighed. *God help me, but I love him. I love Athaulf. A Visigoth!* And she knew there was a connection between them that would never be broken, knew he was thinking of her, was certain his night would be just as disrupted as hers, because Athaulf the Barbarian loved her, too!

She clasped her hands together. *Lord, give me strength—wisdom! Oh, why must I be tested so?*

Silence. There was no sign, no answer here.

She took a deep breath and rose from her bed, heading for the balcony, intent on gazing at God's glory, the starry night sky.

*

Holding a glass of wine, Gigi stood in the middle of their bedroom and studied the gorgeous frescoes, which reminded her of the art she'd seen in Pompeii. Every inch of wall was painted with scenes from antiquity, as if one were looking through windows at gods and nymphs, ladies in Grecian gowns and athletes at their games.

Magnus came up behind her and wrapped his arms around her waist.

"Careful, don't spill my wine," she laughed.

He kissed her neck and took the glass, one arm still around her. "There," he said, placing it on a table, then pulling her tight.

She snuggled against him. "You're so good to me."

"You deserve it."

"So does Placidia. Did you see how she and Athaulf looked at each other?" she asked. "Could it possibly be? Could it possibly happen? She talked of running away before leaving Ravenna. What if she came with us? It would be so perfect."

Magnus disengaged his arms and walked under the arches leading to the balcony. "It can't happen."

Gigi was surprised by this curt remark. "Why not?"

He spun around and faced her. "Because she is a Roman princess, Gigi. A Roman *lady*."

Stunned, Gigi stared at her husband. "I thought you admired the Visigoths. I thought you felt they were equals."

"Not if they plan on rutting with our women!"

"Is that what *we* do, then?" Gigi fumed. "I thought we made love, but now you're telling me when we barbarians mingle with you Romans it can only mean rutting. Is that so?"

"That's not what I said. You're not a barbarian."

"Well, I'm no Roman! And it *is* what you implied. Athaulf is a decent, honorable, and, might I add, desperately lonely man. His wife died years ago, and he's shouldered the responsibility of raising their six children alone. I've never seen him running after skirts. That's not what he cares about. He didn't look at her like he wanted to rut. He looked like he wanted to fold Placidia into his arms and care for her for the rest of his days."

Magnus sat down, his elbows on his knees, and stared at the floor.

Gigi touched his cheek, then put a hand on his shoulder. "He looked at her, Magnus, like you look at me—like you looked at me that day in the garden—like you looked at me when you first arrived in the Visigoth camp—overwhelmed, deeply in love, yet unfailingly honorable."

His head dropped, and he nodded. "You're right. He's as good a man as any Roman."

She lightly ran her fingers through his hair. "You know, you still look at me like that, and it takes my breath away every time. Just before Placidia left the banquet tonight, they both looked like I feel when we have to be apart—like they were being stabbed through the heart with a molten knife."

"I was wrong to say what I did. Forgive me, but I claimed her as my special charge, watched over her, loved her as a brother since she was barely old enough to talk."

"Little sisters grow up, Magnus," Gigi said softly, "and if they're lucky, one day they fall in love with a wonderful man, and you have to let them go."

He smiled. "So wise, for one so beautiful. Did you have a meddling big brother?"

The words struck hard, and Gigi rose and moved to the balcony, looking out over the darkened city. Her other life was so remote, so very far away.

"No. No brother. Just my parents and my grandfather," she murmured. "I still miss them, every day."

"I know." Magnus picked her up in his arms and carried her to bed. Lying beside her, he brushed away her hair, tracing her chin, her nose, her mouth. "You are Victoria's greatest gift to me. You are my greatest strength. We are each other's family now."

"Making new memories together." She smiled and started undoing his clothes. "All day I have been looking forward to making love to you in this beautiful room, with all these luxurious things," she said as she wriggled out of her robe.

"You are." He kissed her again.

"That may be so, but I find the room means nothing to me," she whispered, and their gazes locked. "You are all that matters."

"My sentiment exactly, but let's not overlook such an opportunity. There is the tub, and the fires are lit to heat the water whenever we desire to use it. For now," he reached over and picked up Gigi's glass of wine, "I will concentrate on how I might create a need for the bath."

He trickled some of the wine between her breasts, then leaned in and licked away the rivulet that had run down and pooled in her navel. He tipped the glass again and a few more drops fell on her mound, tickling and lighting a fire between her legs. When his head lowered again, Gigi moaned with pleasure.

Magnus set the glass aside and opened a tiny carafe he'd tucked within the folds of the bed, and pulled out the stopper.

Gigi reached for him, but he shook his head. "Not yet. It is time you had another massage." He drizzled oil scented with lavender and camphor on each breast, then across her stomach and hips. Putting the carafe aside, he spread the oil in slow, firm circles, rubbing his thumbs across her nipples, then kissing them when they rose, fanning her flames down below.

He turned his attention to her hips, spreading and kneading the oil into every fold and crevice, exploring, touching, tasting. The camphor created a heat of its own, and Gigi couldn't help but writhe beneath his attentions.

When at last he rose over her, she reached for the oil and poured some into the palm of her hand. As he hovered, watching, she spread oil on him, working it in with both hands, cupping him, gently pulling, then pumping up and down, faster and faster.

With a strangled groan, he whisked her hands aside and plunged into her, both of them gasping at the impact. Time and luxury lost all meaning as they moved together, finding their rhythm, seeking their bliss.

Sensing her peak was near, Gigi thrust her hips against his, again and again, wanting all of him inside her, hard, pummeling. They cried out together, a sustained, searing explosion of release.

Magnus collapsed beside her, but after only a few minutes of rest, he took her chin and turned her face to his. "You are all that matters," he softly repeated. "I have been truly blessed to find one such as you. And if Placidia can also find such happiness, then who am I to question her choice? I will celebrate their union, should it come to that, no matter his bloodline."

"I love you, Magnus." Gigi moved over him, kissing him, taking her time, making him beg for more.

The embers had died, and the bath water was cool by the time they used it, but, after the heat of that night, they didn't mind.

*

Athaulf stood in the wine cellar of the House of Livia and scanned the selection. He picked an amphora painted in the Greek style of black and orange, depicting beautiful women dancing amid grape vines. He turned to go, but the servant who'd followed him in, and bobbed and shifted while he'd made his choice, seemed ready to expire from a nervous condition.

"Have I taken a special vintage?" Athaulf asked pleasantly. "I would not want anything too valuable, as I am no expert in wine."

"No, no, my lord. It is a white wine called Tears of Christ. This vintage is good, but not extraordinary," he squeaked.

"Tears of Christ?"

"It is said Our Lord wept for the wickedness of Pompeii and grape vines sprang forth in the region."

Athaulf wanted to scoff at this Catholic notion of Jesus's divinity, but he was too tired to argue on the side of his Arian Christian faith, and besides, he thought, each to his own.

"My lord, is there something else you desire?"

"No."

The man shrugged. "It is my duty to serve you. Let me open it, and I'll bring it to your room with something savory, which will bring out its greatest attributes. Does that please?"

"Fine." Athaulf handed the amphora over. "But make it quick, and no fancy goblets. An ordinary mug will do me well enough."

"Indeed, indeed. Most assuredly, my lord. Ordinary, as you say. I shall be back straight away."

The little man scampered off, and Athaulf returned to his room. Several oil lamps lit the interior, and he took a moment to look at the brightly painted walls, the deeply padded bed and its silk draping, the pair of lemon trees in pots, and the multitude of other luxurious tidbits. He felt awkward here, gritty and uncouth. He'd never considered himself that way before, never thought about it at all, until now.

Until her.

A tap at the door broke his train of thought. "Enter."

The man bobbed in, all smiles and bows, and set an alabaster tray on the table. Varieties of cheese and sliced peaches were artfully arranged on a plate beside an open flask and mug, the set made of beautiful blue glass. Athaulf guessed the ordinary crockery was actually quite costly. And the peaches! He had tasted them but a few times in his life. They were exotic and very expensive, the food of foreign kings.

The servant poured the wine. "Will you be requiring anything else, my lord?"

Athaulf took a sip. It was dry, pleasing enough, like every other wine. "Fine, no, nothing more. That will be it for the evening."

"Ah," the servant said, holding a finger up, "before I forget. Sometimes we must point out, I should say, you may well, er, as to one's normal functions, I would be remiss if I did not make you aware of some of the modern conveniences that have been installed in the House of Livia. Quite different, I should imagine, than living in the wild, in a tent."

Athaulf frowned and watched the servant bustle toward a door he'd not previously noticed, since its outline was incorporated into the wall's design.

"Here, my lord, is the indoor latrine, and here," he held up a stick with a small sea sponge affixed to one end, "this is your swab—for cleansing. The vinegar bucket for rinsing is just below, and there is a small fountain of running water for your needs. Please press the lever here by the sink, and water will issue from the fish's mouth."

Athaulf looked at the golden fish faucet and frowned at the ridiculous waste of treasure. "Did you think I'd planned on using one of the potted trees?" he asked irritably.

The servant stopped moving and looked terrified, perhaps realizing he'd stepped over his bounds. "No, my lord, no. Of course not. Not in the least."

"That will be all," Athaulf said, and the man hurried out the door.

Athaulf stared after him for a moment, then took off his tunic, balled it up, and threw it against the wall, admitting to himself he might well have used the potted trees had he found nothing else. The likelihood of his searching the room for a hidden privy would have been slight. *Think, idiot! If you are but a crass barbarian to a Roman slave, what then to a princess of the Empire?*

He grabbed the flask and sloshed some wine into the mug. He drank the contents in one swallow, willing Placidia's image from his mind, but found it an impossible task. Her dark eyes had crinkled at the corners when she smiled at him. Her hair, bound up in a knot on her head, so curly and lustrous-black, bounced when she argued her point.

How long was it? If unbound, would her locks fall between her shoulder blades, or perhaps to the small of her back? Might they fall even farther?

"Stop it!" he grumbled, then poured out more wine, wishing it were beer. He recalled her slender fingers gracefully holding her glass, bringing food to her lips. He squeezed his eyes shut. Great God, he could see them so clearly, those lips! How they moved when she spoke, when she smiled and laughed, or how they closed around a morsel.

Gasts! he cursed to himself in Visigoth, then threw the mug and it crashed against the wall, shattering into a thousand pieces. He watched as the wine trickled down the face of a fancy-painted flowering tree filled with birds. It was a mess. Perfect. Now the oaf-barbarian had ruined her wall. Coming here was nothing short of torture!

Athaulf took up the flask and went onto the balcony with its row of columns, gazing up at their ornate carvings. Such splendor. He looked out over the vista of the ancient, imperial city. Taking a swig, he leaned against a column, his eyes wandering across the intricate geometrical pattern on the mosaic floor, over the marble balustrade, then out again, drinking in the wine and the view.

This was her world. This was her. Beautiful beyond measure. An agony of desire, worlds beyond his reach. How she had looked at him! He tilted his head back, banging it lightly against the stone. As though no one else lived. That was how she looked at him. He could tell. He could feel her desire reaching out to him from across the table. It had taken all of his self-control not to throw everyone out and embrace her the moment they'd first been introduced.

Suddenly, unbidden images of her despicable brother came

to mind, and Athaulf found it hard to believe the two could possibly be blood-kin. One, the very essence of stupidity, evil and debauched, and the other, the very essence of kindness, gifted and warm, her heart gentle as a lover's kiss.

He took another swig, and a tiny movement caught his eye. Lowering the bottle, he swallowed, realizing he could see her palace in the distance. There was someone moving on the balcony, someone in a pale gown. He stepped forward. *Could it be?* His heart thumped like a battle drum.

The figure turned toward him and stopped, but the distance was too great to be sure if she was returning his gaze.

Placidia! He wanted to call out her name.

Almost immediately she was gone, the balcony empty, and Athaulf stood transfixed, for as she'd turned away, the moonlight had danced off the dark curls cascading down her back, her long tresses swaying as she moved, grazing the lovely curve of her bottom.

*

The sculptor was covered in marble dust, chiseling, chiseling. The bust was starting to take shape, already hinting at the man's genius, but Honorius yawned in boredom. He hated the heavenward gaze of his statue's cold, marble eyes, but it was necessary, reminding the plebs he was God's Chosen One.

As the artist tenderly wiped the stone with his fingers, stroking the cold marble as though it were a woman's flesh, Honorius scoffed and motioned for Britomartis and Adriadne. They hurried forward to do his bidding.

He pulled Adriadne close, kissing her throat, her skin smooth, warm, and scented with rose water. "Massage our neck and shoulders," he said. He felt Britomartis nestle against him. "And you," he grabbed hold of her shapely behind, "you little minx, we desire a leg tickle."

Giggling, the girls playfully struggled away from him, then started to massage. He closed his eyes, their fingers soft upon his body, exactly the way he liked it. He reveled in the ripples of pleasure running up and down his legs, the deeper caresses erasing the tension in his back.

"My lord," Britomartis whispered, "I think you would purr if you could."

Honorius laughed. "Where is Rutilius Namatianus?"

"I am here," he called from the corridor.

Honorius didn't bother to open his eyes. "We are bored. Recite your most recent poem for us."

There was silence. Only the *tap, tap* of the sculptor's chisel filled the air.

Honorius opened his eyes. Namatianus stood there, gaping like an idiot.

"My lord, it is not yet finished," the man protested. "Perhaps I—"

Honorius frowned. "We care not. Recite what you have written so far."

Namatianus nodded, breathed deeply, and then intoned:

"Hear, O beautiful Queen of the World which is thine,

O Rome now received among the celestial spheres!

Hear, O Mother of Men and Mother of Gods,

Thou who, through thy temples,

Make us feel less distant from the heavens!

We sing of thee and always of thee—

As long as the Fates allow, we sing.

Thou hast created for people of every country a single fatherland;

For lawless peoples it was great fortune to be subjugated by thee.

In offering the vanquished the equality of thy rights,

Thou hast made a city of what once was the world."

Honorius was suddenly aware the girls' fingers had stopped, the sculptor's chisel was still. This pleased him, for he too was enchanted by the words.

"*Urbem fecisti quod prius orbis erat*," he said, whispering the final line. Thou hast made a city of what once was the world.

How true it was! If only the cursed Visigoths could understand.

Namatianus cleared his throat. "As I said before, the poem is not yet finished. I plan to honor you in the next stanzas, *Venerabilis*, for you are the personification of Rome's glory, come to life."

Honorius yawned again. As the massage resumed, he realized he was feeling quite tired. He bade the girls cease and started to rise.

"Forgive the intrusion, O most excellent Honorius."

He turned as the captain of his guards ushered in a stranger carrying a wooden box. The man went down on one knee.

"My lord," the captain said, "this courier has a gift for you, sent by a citizen of Rome."

Honorius's pulse quickened. Those were code words, meaning it was over, done. "Open the box," he ordered eagerly.

The man looked at the women and hesitated.

Honorius tapped his foot. "Open it!"

"As you wish, Your Majesty." He pulled off the lid, reached inside, and brought forth a small head, that of a child.

Honorius ignored the sound of the chisel clattering to the floor, the screams of the girls, the horrified gasp of Rutilius Namatianus. He bent closer, unmoved by the stench of decay, fascinated by what had happened to Eucherius's face.

The boy looked strange, wizened, like an old monkey. Ah, what to do with such a dreadfully wonderful thing?

Rubbing his chin, Honorius recalled an old saying, *If I cannot bend Heaven, I shall move Hell.*

Clapping his hands, he said, "Pickle it! If Alaric the Uncouth dares to cause any more trouble, we shall send this to him, reminding him of our power."

*

Placidia gazed at the leaden morning sky, its gloomy promise matching the feel of her heart. She turned to Gigi. "I miss you already. I wish you could stay longer," she said, hugging her. "Magnus, take good care of her."

They bowed and moved off, and Athaulf approached. Placidia looked into his eyes and trembled at his masculine beauty.

"My lady," he spoke quietly, "it was my greatest pleasure to meet you, for you have opened my eyes to what is good and fine about Rome. Would that I could stay longer." He took her hand and kissed it. "Would that I could stay forever."

He released her and sighed.

Her skin still tingled with the memory of his touch. "Athaulf," she whispered, realizing his name was already precious to her. "Athaulf, we cannot leave it here. We *must* meet again."

He looked startled and then gazed at her eyes, her lips. Placidia felt the rush of her blood, a deep surge of desire. Her hand moved toward him. She wanted to touch his face, but he checked her move with his eyes and pulled back.

"We shall meet again, if God wills it. Farewell, sweet Placidia."

She watched him leave with the others, her throat tight with emotion. It was the first time he had spoken her name. She prayed to all the saints in Heaven it would not be the last.

Chapter 5

Accompanied by her maid, Persis, and her few remaining bodyguards, Placidia trudged back up the Scalae Caci leading to her palace, pushing at dripping curls escaping from beneath her *palla*. It had been raining for days, and the weather was unseasonably cold. What were they going to do? When was Honorius going to pay the city's ransom? She wrapped the sodden cloak closer about her shoulders and shook her head, miserable. She was a fool! Her brother hadn't even bothered to respond to her pleas, other than to say it was none of his doing, and Rome would have to find her own way out of this disaster.

Between the two of them, she and Attalus had managed to browbeat the Senate into gradually doling out what was left of the grain supply. Alaric had cut off all deliveries into Rome, rationing the food allowance by half, then by two-thirds when he learned some amount of grain was still to be found within the walls. Every Friday for the past month, Placidia had gone to different storage facilities, begging the people there to share what they were given, share what little they had stashed away with their families, their neighbors, those most vulnerable. And Placidia was adamant her household should receive no more food or fuel for heating and cooking than any other.

But despite careful planning, strict rationing, and city-wide cooperation, everything was running dangerously short, and no amount of money could buy what wasn't there to be had. Where once meat and fish had been plentiful, now none could be found, and it was becoming apparent dogs, cats, even rodents, were disappearing from the streets and homes.

Many men had already escaped, singly and stealthily, abandoning wives and children. Some people left openly, throwing their lot in with the Visigoths, either for survival or out of ideological reasoning, and many slaves had vanished as well.

When she reached home, there were three pitiful old women sitting outside the gates. When they saw her, their thin arms rose up as one, their weak, crackly voices begging for food.

"Placidia, please." "*Domina*, help us." "We have been left to die." "*Nobilissima Puella*, please help us."

Placidia crouched down, taking their feeble hands in hers. "I haven't much to offer, only some olives, cheese, and stale bread. But we will divvy up what little we have, and at least you may come in out of the rain and sit by our fire," she smiled apologetically, "although we have but a small amount of wood left. Please, you are welcome at our hearth." She glanced at her bodyguards, who looked angry and disinclined to assist. Even Persis hung back.

Placidia frowned. "If you don't care to share your portions with these women, then they may take mine, but I insist you bring them inside!"

Their expressions were petulant, but they all helped, and soon everyone was settled and the doors were closed against the frigid, damp air.

*

The rain drummed loudly against the roof tiles, keeping Placidia awake. It was late, and she was so very tired. Hunger hurt more than just her body, it hurt her mind with its ceaseless torments, the wretched cravings. *When would this be over? When?*

Suddenly, a loud thump on the balcony jolted her upright in bed.

Her ladies hurried in. "What was that?" Elpidia asked.

"Perhaps a bird has crashed into the side of the palace?" Placidia suggested. She got up and followed the women to the balcony. Together, they pulled open the heavy curtains and peeked out. A large burlap sack was lying against the wall.

"Stay here," Elpidia told them. "Let me take a look."

Placidia sent Persis to help when Elpidia struggled to lift and carry the sack by herself. They dragged it inside and closed the curtains.

"The balcony is so high. How could someone throw such a heavy thing?" Placidia asked. She reached out to untie the knot securing the sack.

"No, don't!" Elpidia grabbed her arm. "Someone climbed up and left it here, then fled. What if it holds something horrible?"

"Dear Lord!" Placidia backed away, suddenly fearful of what they might find.

Elpidia's mouth was tight as she gazed at the curtains. "We have fewer guards on duty these days. They must have stopped patrolling the grounds. I will go out directly and talk to them about this." She started for the door. "Do not open the sack, Placidia. Please! I shall call for a guard."

Placidia was about to nod when she detected an aroma, something sweet and wonderful. She looked down at the sack, suddenly unafraid. "Elpidia, wait. Can't you smell them?"

Both Persis and Elpidia stared at her.

"Smell what?" the nurse asked.

"Figs and dates! The bag must be full of—"

"No, my lady, stop!" Elpidia yelled. "Leave it be until I return with help."

Ignoring her, Placidia tore open the sack. "Oh, look!" Excitedly, she plunged her hand inside and drew out kernels of spelt, wanting to devour it raw. "There is grain and also dates, nuts and figs, even cheese. Oh, my God, food, someone has brought us food."

"But who . . . ?" Persis reached out, then pulled back. "What if it contains poison?"

Before she could stop herself, Placidia popped some nuts and a dried fig into her mouth, chewing slowly, savoring the explosion of nearly forgotten flavors. She waited a moment, then smiled. No convulsions or loss of sight. No stomach pains.

Elpidia crossed herself and nibbled at a date, while Persis wolfed down some cheese, but after Placidia swallowed a second helping of nuts, she looked around guiltily. "We cannot do this. We cannot hoard such a gift. It would be selfish and terribly un-Christian, unforgivable."

Persis's faced reddened as she reluctantly put the cheese back into the sack. "You are right, my lady."

Elpidia swallowed and hung her head. "What should we do?"

Placidia grabbed the sack of spelt and hoisted it, testing its weight. "There must be fifteen *libres* of grain, not counting the other food. We have enough to make many, many bowls of hot *puls* with this amount." Her mouth watered at the memory of porridge laced with honey, despite the fact there was no honey to be found in Rome these days.

Placidia, be grateful for what has been given!

Then something made her pause, something in the air, something so transient, so faint, but compelling and unforgettable.

Astonished, she put her hands to her face. Leather and lavender. Unblinking, mouth open in surprise, she looked at the women. "I know who brought this."

*

Placidia felt hungry and tired, her hands cold, her heart colder still. Six weeks and counting since she'd sent word to Honorius, since he'd refused to become involved. Four weeks since Athaulf had first smuggled in food, but the deliveries had tapered off, and it was ten days since the last one.

Why? Where was he? Her eyes misted, and she feared he no longer cared.

She walked to the balcony, parted the heavy curtains and gazed out. The weather was wet and miserable, winter's fury come early, and innumerable diseases ran rampant in the city, killing more than they ought, because of everyone's deteriorating strength.

Shivering, she hurried back inside. Warming her hands over a brazier, she breathed in the heady, sweet scent given off by her last, precious hoard of stone pine, then went to her mirror and studied her wavy reflection in the polished bronze. Placidia could make out the dark circles under her eyes, the sharp prominence of her cheekbones matching the increasingly skeletal look of her body. Despite Athaulf's gifts, she was losing weight. They were all losing weight.

She'd shared his bounty as best she could with her servants and Attalus, and gave out bits and morsels amongst the weakest beggars in the street. But she had to be careful, knowing if it got out the palace was hoarding food, they would be overrun, and possibly killed.

Her mind flitted toward a memory of hazel eyes flecked with green. Passionate eyes. But she reminded herself she could not abandon her people and run to him. No, she had to stay in Rome, even die, if that was God's will, if that was how hard Honorius's heart remained, despite her pleas.

"My lady?" Persis asked, as she and Elpidia entered, bringing in Placidia's warmest night shift and blankets. "How were the gladiatorial contests? Did they amuse? Were the people happy to have something else to think about, beyond finding food?"

Elpidia grumbled at this, and Placidia looked at her for a moment before raising her arms to be undressed. "It was a disaster, and yet the Senate wants to do it again next week." She paused as Elpidia slipped the shift over her head. "I cannot abide such violence, but I was overruled by Attalus and the other senators. I closed my eyes to the blood." Her voice broke and she swallowed hard, willing away the images of sodden, red sand, of bodies cut to pieces. "And, do you know, with each death the crowds chanted, 'Food, food, food,' and we tried to ignore them, pretending we didn't understand what they were saying. By the end, though, it . . . it was horrible . . . they were howling, insisting the dead be handed over as part of the food rationing."

Persis recoiled. "No, they didn't!"

As Placidia's eyes welled, Elpidia patted her arm, trying to comfort her.

"Heaven help us," Placidia said, "but the whispers of cannibalism are true! They didn't even care that such evil desires were given voice so publicly. Everyone was clamoring for the bodies. If not for the guards, I think they would have started tearing at each other."

Someone knocked at the door.

"Senator Attalus has just come in, *Domina*," Leontius spoke from behind the closed door. "He begs your forgiveness and wishes to speak with you."

"Tell him I will meet him in my study immediately." Placidia sighed and stood, squaring her shoulders. "I am sorry, Elpidia. I don't care if I'm being indecent, but I haven't the strength of body or will to get redressed."

"Here, put on your *palla*. With this and your heavy shift you'll be fine, my dear. You are always a proper lady. Go ahead."

The hallways echoed with their footsteps as Placidia followed her steward. The palace seemed so empty these days. Many had deserted her or died. Even the three old women she'd brought in were dead, each having lasted less than a week. Since then, dozens in her household had succumbed, and many more had simply vanished. Nevertheless, it wouldn't do to look as defeated as she felt, not even to Attalus.

Leontius opened the door to her study, and she went inside. With one look at Attalus's haggard expression, she wished she'd never come to Rome, wished she'd never been born a princess, wished all these burdens and worries had never been placed at her doorstep. She was only seventeen, after all. She started. No, she was eighteen! Her birthday had been missed, not celebrated or even remembered. God in Heaven, what more could she possibly—

Placidia checked herself. Even now, the spoiled princess lurked within.

She sighed. What grief was Attalus going to add to her heart tonight? By his dour looks, it was something momentous and grim.

Placidia lifted her chin and looked directly into his eyes. "Attalus, what news?"

He bowed. "I am sorry to have to tell you, but this afternoon Serena was arrested while sneaking in through the Quirinalis Gate. It is not the first time this was observed. She has been watched since the murder of her son, although at first we did it for protective measures. However, soon we observed her frequent comings and goings. It is said she brought in contraband—food to be precise. We are not sure how she acquires it. But it is either through the, er, sale of herself, or perhaps she is giving the Visigoths information. At any rate, she is having extensive dealings with them."

"With King Alaric?" Placidia paused, then blurted, "Not Athaulf!"

"No. The tents of the barbarian leaders are not located in the area she frequents," Attalus replied. "But there is another, one Sergeric by name, who is known to be corrupt, even disloyal, when it serves his purpose. He has often been seen hanging around the gate. We have reason to believe it is with Sergeric that Serena meets and comes by her food."

Placidia sat on the closest couch, staring at the floor, on the verge of abandoning all hope, for she feared what was coming. "And what have they decided is to be done with my cousin?"

"The Senate has decreed Serena be brought before the people at next week's games," Attalus said flatly, "where she will be charged as a traitor to Rome. The crowd will also be reminded of what she did at the Temple of Rhea years ago, when she stole the offerings to the goddess, just in case anyone has forgotten that travesty. Then they will ask what sentence they would demand for her crimes."

"They will ask the public? Oh, Lord Almighty, I fear they will have no mercy! Will it be stoning, do you think?" Placidia whispered. "To be carried out immediately?"

"The sentence will be meted out on the spot, certainly, but we must anticipate the plebs will demand much worse than stoning."

"Dear God. Might she be burned?"

Attalus shrugged. "There is one more thing."

"What?" she asked weakly. "What more can there possibly be?"

"The Senate insists on your presence."

Placidia groaned.

"And they want you to publicly give final approval to whatever sentence is demanded. They feel it is the only way for you to remain untarnished by Serena's guilt, and the only way to keep order."

*

The gray skies hung low, and the wind promised more rain. Placidia snuggled into her fur cape. Resigned to the inevitable, she sat in the imperial stands of the Flavian Amphitheater, surrounded by several senators, Attalus behind her. The sweet smoke of stone pine wafted from several huge braziers, set around the grounds of the great coliseum, not for warmth, but to mask the odors of gore and death.

But on this day, Placidia thought, *by my orders none have died, and it is not necessary to cleanse the air, at least not yet.* She stared out at the arena floor. Six pairs of gladiators had battled over the course of the afternoon, the winners receiving laudatory palm fronds and pouches of gold. The rain had held off, and she sensed the games were a success, despite the restlessness of the crowd, still seething for blood.

Now, only one event was left to be played out. Placidia quailed at what she was about to witness, her participation a necessary evil.

There was a clatter of gates at one of the field entrances, and all eyes sought the reason. Placidia turned toward the disturbance and saw several legionnaires. They stood rigidly at attention, and behind them, two more legionnaires holding one diminutive woman with long, dark tresses falling loose over her shoulders.

Serena. The moment had come.

People started to hiss and boo as she was led out and made to stand alone in the center of the arena, her hands bound behind her back. She was clothed in a shift too light for the weather, and despite the cold, her chin was high, Placidia noted, a look of utter disdain her only expression.

Near the front railing, the announcer rose in full make-up and blond wig, his clothing gaudy and crass, in the theatrical style. He lifted a hand to quiet the crowd, waiting a moment until everyone grew still. "We have before us, Serena, wife of the traitor General Stilicho!" he called, his voice dulcet, yet loud and clear, a wonder of contradictions.

The crowd roared in blood-thirsty anticipation, and Placidia closed her eyes, feeling shaken and ill. Grabbing the arms of her throne, she took several gulps of air and prayed for strength, for a way out of this madness.

It grew quiet again, and Placidia opened her eyes.

"Serena was caught smuggling food into the city," the announcer continued, "for her private and personal use, which she received through consort with the very enemy that hems us in and starves us these many weeks, and even at this moment, ongoing." He pointed at Serena, who glared back. "We also deem it prudent to remind you, this woman is the very same who, some years back, made a mockery of the Temple of Rhea, the Goddess of the Old Ways, and still venerated by many among you. Serena desecrated Rhea's temple and stole such gifts as had been given in tribute."

Placidia saw something fly out from the seats behind Serena, striking her cousin on the shoulder with enough force to open the skin and cause bleeding. Cheers rocked the stadium as Serena stumbled, but she managed to keep her footing, haughty, angry, ever defiant.

The announcer raised his hand again. As silence fell once more, Placidia realized she was still gripping her chair. She let go and sat back, her fingers aching.

"Citizens of Rome," the announcer cried out. "Since the guilt of this woman is beyond question, we have decided to ask you, the people against whom this crime was committed, to bring sentence upon her!"

Jeers and applause. The stands thundered with the stamping of feet.

"What is your sentence?"

"Death! Death! Death!"

Placidia remained still, letting only her eyes move over the scene. People shook their fists and screamed obscenities; some threw whatever they could find, the missiles raining down on the field. Several found their mark, but Serena remained standing and unbowed.

The announcer waved his arms for calm, then, when the voices subsided enough he bellowed, "By what means?"

There was no deciphering the responses, since none were the same, but everyone continued to roar.

He waved his arms again. "Stoning?"

Roars.

"Burning?"

Thunderous noise.

"Disemboweling?"

Placidia could hardly hear the man, and there was no way to make sense of what the crowd preferred. He said something else, but his voice was lost in the din, and finally he nodded, then motioned for quiet. As a hush fell over the crowd, he suddenly turned with a flourish and faced Placidia.

The brusqueness of the move took her by surprise, and she sat there, cold with dread.

"Stand," Attalus whispered in her ear.

With difficulty, Placidia shrugged off her cape and rose. "What is the people's decision?" she asked, her voice sounding strange and throaty, as if it belonged to another.

"Aelia Galla Placidia, Most Noble Princess of Rome and the Empire, the people have chosen beheading, to be carried out immediately!"

Placidia blinked several times, trying to manage her surprise. She hadn't heard a single voice call out for so humane a method of execution, and she guessed Attalus had something to do with it, although he bore Serena no goodwill.

Placidia focused on her cousin, and Serena stared back with a smirk, unmoving, daring her to pronounce condemnation, mocking her failure to do so.

How she hated evil, loathsome Serena! Placidia reminded herself of all the wrongs this woman had committed in her lifetime, reminded herself she was every bit the craven monster Honorius was, reminded herself this woman was uncaring, vengeful, and utterly without compassion.

Compassion.

Placidia tried to calm her breathing as she looked into eyes that would soon be without life. Whatever Serena's faults, Placidia fervently wished she could show her compassion, even now, but that was not an option.

Instead, she drew in a deep breath and raised her fist with an extended thumb, drawing a line over her throat in the *pollice verso*, the death signal, final, so very final.

"Let the people's decision be carried out!" she ordered.

The noise throbbed in Placidia's ears, pulsated across the arena, as two legionnaires grasped Serena's arms and forced her to her knees. A third took hold of the ends of her hair from the front, pulling it all forward, forcing her face down and exposing the nape of her neck.

Lightning flashed across the sky and thunder ripped through the heavens. A storm was upon them. Huge raindrops began to pelt the arena.

Another flash of light, this time daylight on blade, and the stroke descended with a terrible force.

Placidia's legs gave way and she almost fell, but Attalus caught her in time, holding her up before the people, to witness this last, Serena's end, for the sake of the Eternal City, for Rome, her Rome.

Chapter 6

Three days without rain—it was like heaven. Wrapped in a sheepskin cloak, Gigi walked through the lanes between tents, choosing her footing carefully. The morning had dawned overcast and bitterly cold. Frost coated everything, and the puddles had all iced over. If this chill stayed around, and the rains came back, they would be knee-deep in snow in no time. And what would that mean for Rome? For Placidia?

Damn this weather! Damn obstinate men! Triple damn that bastard Honorius for ignoring everything that's going on!

She made her way to a rise topped with a lone cypress, her breath making little clouds before it disappeared. Gigi looked at the vista, Rome, so beautiful as it sparkled in the morning light— so terrible, too, and in such agony.

Gigi put her flute to her lips and played some arpeggios to warm up. Then, raising her eyes to the great cityscape, she played an original piece she had developed over the past weeks. She thought of it as her "Ode to Rome" and hoped it could be heard all the way into the city, to encourage and give hope, to let them know they were not forgotten.

Then, almost as soon as she'd begun, something caught her eye and the notes faltered, then stopped. Standard flags bobbed in the distance. People and wagons were traveling up the road. There was a delegation coming from the city!

Gigi started down the hill, slipping, stumbling, but managing to stay up. When she finally got to the flats, she ran full out, heedless of the ruts and frozen puddles. Trying to catch her breath, she arrived at Alaric's tent with many others, just as the delegation came into view.

King Alaric was already standing beside the great central fire pit, the official meeting place. Alaric's elderly foster-mother, Randegund, stood on his left, her birth children, Queen Verica and Athaulf, on her right, while Magnus, Sergeric and several of the other captains waited farther off. The welcoming committee.

Just then, Randegund's gaze strayed toward Gigi, who shivered beneath the woman's icy-blue glare. The old witch hated all things Roman, and marrying Magnus had put Gigi squarely in the enemy camp. She had tried to stay away from Randegund, but the woman was frequently in Alaric's company and avoiding her proved impossible. At first Gigi hadn't understood why Alaric kept Randegund so close, but then she'd pieced together the complicated relationship between the two; not only had Randegund taken him in when he was orphaned as a child, she'd given him her only daughter's hand in marriage. It was still hard for Gigi to believe sweet Verica and noble Athaulf were scary Randegund's biological children.

With a last, defiant look at the witch, Gigi edged her way along the fringes of the crowd. She found a decent spot to one side, where she could see all the faces, and hopefully hear something.

"Jolie! Jolie!" a little voice cried out.

Gigi looked down, surprised to see Berga, Alaric and Verica's youngest, hopping up and down. She grinned at Berga's continued use of the alias Gigi had first given the Visigoths—Angelina Jolie. It had been a spur-of-the-moment decision so Honorius's spies would never make the connection with the fugitive slave they knew as Gigiperrin.

"Help me up, Jolie."

"Shhh, Berga." Gigi rumpled the girl's hair. "This is very important. Your parents are going to have an important meeting. We must be quiet."

"We told her that!" two insistent voices said in unison.

Gigi looked behind her. The twin boys were there, looking annoyed with their sister. She knelt down and motioned for Berga to climb on her back, then glanced at the twins. "Go to the front to watch, but come right back here afterward to get your sister."

They started to complain, but when Gigi threw them a look, they quickly wriggled past onlookers to a prime location.

A murmur of astonishment swept the crowd and Gigi rose with Berga, straining to see.

Berga pointed and started to giggle. "They're funny looking. Those men have naked faces. They must get cold as girls in the wintertime."

Gigi drew in her breath at the sight of Priscus Attalus and several other Romans. Although dressed in their finest senatorial regalia, they looked haggard and thin. Attalus was in the worst shape, his face ashen and pinched, the fringe of hair around his bald pate now snow-white. She could see the nubs of his shoulder bones poking up against his toga.

What was this about? She struggled through the mass of people, straining for a better spot. "Berga, you absolutely cannot say a word, no giggling, not one sound. Promise?"

"Promise," Berga breathed in her tiniest voice, right next to Gigi's ear.

"Good girl."

Once at the front, Gigi stood in amazement. Behind the cluster of Roman senators came dozens of large wagons, each pulled by legionnaires and guarded by others marching three deep on both sides, and running the entire length of the convoy.

" . . . all the worldly riches left to Rome," Attalus was saying, his tone low and shaded with desperation. "They avail us not, since they cannot sustain life, so we give them freely, in exchange for a lifting of the siege. Rome asks you, noble King Alaric of the Visigoths, please, allow us to purchase our freedom, our very lives, but know that we ask this as citizens only, and do not speak for the Empire, since the Empire has chosen to ignore our plight."

Do it, Alaric, Gigi tried to force her thoughts into his. *Accept the offer.*

"Tell me, Senator Attalus," the king responded calmly, "what have you brought? All the riches of Rome, you say, but I have no need of statues and fancy paintings. You Romans owe me gold and land, and if I don't receive my due, my men shall—"

"What? Your men shall what?" Another senator, a tall, unfamiliar man with a hooked nose, stepped forward. "You forget," he said, frowning, "that the people of Rome are well trained and ready to fight."

Alaric laughed. "And I would remind you that handfuls of wheat are easier to cut than individual stalks. If you dare test us—and I would strongly advise against it!—then we shall have no choice; Visigoth scythes shall reap your Roman blades in one fell swoop."

"Please, please, King Alaric," Attalus said, raising his hands, "we have brought you all we have."

"Bah!" Alaric exclaimed. "I will not give up the siege unless we get all of your gold and silver, as well as all worthy movable property and the barbarian slaves."

"But, but," the hook-nosed senator was stammering now, "what will you leave the citizens of Rome?"

The smile faded from Alaric's face. "Their lives."

A hush descended on the crowd, and Gigi held her breath.

Attalus broke the quiet. "Please, let me show you but a token of the wealth," his hand shook as he motioned to his men, "and I will stay as surety, while you verify the contents of the wagons, if that is what you wish."

Five trunks were placed at Alaric's feet.

"The first ingots in this box are but a hint of what our wagons hold," Attalus said, opening the lid of the nearest one. "There are five thousand *libres* of gold, plus thirty thousand *libres* of silver."

Gigi gasped as excited chatter ran through the people watching, but Alaric's sober expression never wavered.

Attalus opened the next two trunks. "Here are rare silks and spices out of Persia, the lands of the Indus and beyond. In total, four thousand costly tunics and chests filled with every delight of the Orient." He drew a shimmering, red swath of fabric across his arm, his tremors now even more pronounced. "In every hue and texture, the silks will please your women, and so too, your men, while the spices will not only enhance food, they will also cure many ills and afflictions. I have brought you cinnamon, nutmeg—and pepper, over three thousand—"

"Bah! Pepper?" Sergeric scoffed, pretending to sneeze as several of his friends laughed, clearly finding the senator's anxiety highly amusing.

With sympathy, Gigi watched Attalus glance at Magnus, who showed no expression. Then she noticed Randegund glaring at the senator in disdain.

As if sensing her stare, Randegund turned and looked right at Gigi again. Another shiver raced down her spine, for the woman's evil blue eyes seemed paler than before, her gaze colder and more deadly, if that were possible.

"You there," Attalus's voice rose up, and Gigi shifted her gaze, "show them what else we have brought." The senator motioned to the legionnaires of the second and third wagons, who threw back their tarps, revealing heaps of skins and hides, most dyed scarlet.

"In addition to the fine crimson hides for everyday use, we also offer wonderful treasures from Egypt, Namibia, and Nubia: the furs of striped and spotted cats, crocodile hides, all exotic and very expensive," Attalus went on as he held up a gleaming leopard skin. "Their patterns and colors are fantastical and beyond imagining. Use the leather for making boots and shoes, the fur for warmth and decoration."

To Gigi's relief this gift met with great approval, if the sounds of longing around her were any indication.

Attalus opened the fourth box. The senator took out a golden goblet sparkling with jewels and held it out to King Alaric. "A chalice fit for a king, my lord. We have much more here: gold and silver jewelry with gemstones of every size and color, Persian turquoise, and stings of pearls. It is all we have. We have even scraped the gold leaf off statues, columns, ornate carvings and lettering. As I told you . . . in all, five thousand *libres* of gold."

There was little noise this time. Everyone looked tense as Alaric took the goblet and hefted it in his hand. Attalus lifted his chin and gazed at the other leaders, one by one, lastly at Magnus, before he opened the lid on the final box.

"As a token of goodwill, and a gesture to signify that, indeed, innocent Rome has laid herself bare before the steely determination of the Visigoths, and the callous indifference of our emperor in Ravenna, the Imperial Princess, Aelia Galla Placidia, has, as has all Rome, kept nothing for herself. In the most noble of gestures, she gladly hands over all she possesses, for, she said, 'its value is as nothing, compared to the lives of my fellow Romans.'"

What was in the box? Gigi strained for a glimpse as Attalus pulled out an emerald-green silk gown with one hand, and held up an emerald and gold necklace with the other.

Gigi immediately recognized Placidia's things from the night of the dinner. She glanced at Athaulf. He certainly did, too! A noise strangled in his throat, and he started toward Attalus, looking more shaken than angry, but Magnus moved forward and stopped him with a hand on his arm, then whispered something in his ear.

Randegund frowned at Athaulf, while Alaric and Verica looked amazed by his reaction.

Alaric stepped forward, still holding the goblet. "Senator Attalus, I thank you for your generous offerings. Please, take your ease." He looked around and found Gigi, nodding to her. "Magnus's wife will entertain you with her flute, and I shall call for some beer and food. For our part, we shall take leave of you, for we have much to discuss."

As the people dispersed, Athaulf picked up Placidia's box. "I will have no one meddling with anything inside!"

He stalked off to join the other leaders, while Gigi set down Berga, who scampered off to find the queen.

"Come, Senator Attalus," Gigi said. "Come with me."

*

The tent was crowded, already stifling from body heat and shared fervor. Magnus watched as Alaric picked up a skein and started to pour wine into the jewel-encrusted goblet.

"Alaric! No!" Randegund shouted.

Startled, Magnus, Alaric, and the others whirled about to face the old woman.

"Poison!" Her eyes were wide, ablaze with a fearsome blue light. "Do not drink from the goblet!"

Alaric shook his head. "Fear not, Mother. Senator Attalus does not seek to harm, and neither does Galla Placidia—"

"But Honorius does," Magnus interjected as he motioned for the goblet. "I would trust Attalus and Placidia with my life, but," he took the cup and gazed at its interior, wondering if anything had been smeared on the gold, "but Randegund is correct. We must never forget Honorius's arm has a long reach. If you will, I shall take the first drink."

Randegund scowled at Magnus, but Alaric nodded.

Sweat trickled from Magnus's forehead as he swirled the liquid, then put the goblet to his lips. He was glad Gigi wasn't here, in case things went badly.

He took a sip and swallowed, tasting nothing but red, fruity wine.

Heart pounding, Magnus waited a long moment.

Everyone was silent, watching him, until Queen Verica chuckled. "He looks well, does he not—and he got the first drink! I would ask all here to swear an oath of silence regarding his selfless act, else his wife will be quite vexed, and none of us shall ever hear the end of it."

She gave Magnus a smile, relief shining in her eyes. He handed the goblet back to Alaric.

The king grinned. "Magnus, I am indebted by your audacious act of courage." He turned to Athaulf and his captains. "Any objections to Attalus's offer?"

"I should think so!" Sergeric said as he stepped forward. "My lord, you know he lied. The Roman pigs," he frowned at Magnus, "are holding back. This is *Rome*, after all. Their treasure hoard must be vast, much more than two score of wagons."

Alaric turned to Magnus. "What say you to this, my friend?"

Magnus swallowed hard, his thoughts in turmoil, for he knew the truth. Scrambling for an answer, he opened his mouth to speak, but Athaulf stood and blurted, "Enough! There is enough treasure in the Roman wagons to buy us the whole north of Italia, if a homeland is what we truly seek. We should accept the offer and end the siege."

Surprisingly, the group affirmed this with the banging of swords on shields, and even Verica nodded to Alaric. Only Sergeric scowled.

Alaric raised his hand. "No more discussion? This is it?" he asked. "Well then, I declare the siege over, and our next move shall be to the north. The noose is around Honorius's neck now, so let us ride to Ravenna and draw it tight." He turned to one of the sentries. "You there, go and fetch Attalus."

As people began to file out of the tent, Magnus felt a touch on his sleeve and turned. Randegund stood there. "If the cup had been poisoned," she said, "you would now be dead."

He looked straight into her eyes. "Indeed, I would."

"I thank you for protecting him," she added and abruptly walked away.

There was something in the way she'd spoken, a spiteful edge in her tone, which made Magnus smile. He knew what it must have cost her, also knew he could not trust her, could never let down his guard.

She had not changed. She was his oldest enemy, and she would never forgive him for the loss of her husband, whom Magnus had fought beside in battle long ago. Although the death was not his fault, Randegund never wavered in her belief he had been negligent. Her hatred was all still there, despite her show of gratitude.

She was his enemy for life.

*

Gigi sat down across from Attalus as food and beer were placed before him, and he stared at the fare with longing. When he finally lifted his gaze to Gigi, he looked tormented.

"I cannot eat while Rome starves." He pushed the plate and mug away with trembling fingers.

"Senator Attalus," Gigi said, taking his bony hand in hers, "are you well? How is Placidia? She's not ill, is she?"

"She is weak, as are we all. It is strange, what starvation does to a body, but women do better than men, and the princess is young and strong." Attalus sighed. "We have tried to convince Alaric this was not Rome's fault. We know he feels this is his last, best hope to get satisfaction from that horse's ass in Ravenna."

Gigi smiled in agreement.

Attalus spread his hands. "Unfortunately for Rome, the policy is sound. In his place, I would do the same."

A sentry poked his head into the tent. "The king has called for you, Priscus Attalus."

"So soon?" Attalus said, nervously wiping his hands.

Gigi wondered what the hurried summons could mean. Had the Visigoths rejected Rome's offer out of hand?

Within moments, she and Attalus stood at the fire pit again, facing Alaric, Athaulf, Magnus, and the other chieftains, with only Verica and Randegund absent. The crowds had also vanished, the people now going about their daily chores.

Magnus motioned for Gigi to join him. She took his hand and waited, his skin warm, the little squeeze to her fingers his way of telling her it was going to be okay.

She felt her nerves fall away, a sense of calm enveloping her.

The king stepped toward Attalus. "Senator, the siege is lifted. I have already ordered the storage houses opened, and deliveries of food should be on their way as we speak."

"*Yes!*" Gigi exclaimed in English, but only Magnus grinned at her response.

Attalus grasped the king's proffered forearm, tears in his eyes. "May the gods bless you, King Alaric the Wise!"

"May God bless us all," Alaric said.

Athaulf stepped forward with a small item, wrapped in golden silk. "I would have you return this to Galla Placidia," he said to Attalus.

Gigi watched as Athaulf pulled back the edges, revealing the emerald necklace, which he pressed into Attalus's hands.

"No, no," Attalus protested. "Placidia's sacrifice was voluntary, and she insisted you have it."

"But—"

"No! Placidia told me someday she hoped it would be returned to her, but not now." Attalus gave the necklace back to Athaulf and lowered his voice, looking awkward. "She told me . . . "

Gigi strained to hear the senator's next words.

" . . . she awaits the day when you might return this bauble to her neck. She told me she is ever patient, like *Roma aeterna* herself, and she will wait for a new future. She will wait."

*

The curtain rose on the final act, and Honorius smiled. He touched his hair, adjusting his new pearl diadem, knowing he looked magnificent, the pride of the Empire. His smile broadened as he peered at the audience, pleased to see their expressions of awe and rapture.

He raised his sword, flexing his bared muscles, wearing but a loincloth and cloak, like the Greeks of old. Behind him, the stage of his theater had been transformed into a seascape; the air howled with a wind conjured by his court magicians, while an ocean appeared to heave and roar with pounding waves. Britomartis was chained to a column, the marble hidden by layers of plaster, making it look like the famous Siren's Rock off the coast of Sicilia. Honorius gazed at the girl's windblown tresses, her blond hair already damp and clinging to her white skin, which peeked deliciously through the carefully crafted rips in her golden gown.

"Ahhh," he sighed as he winked at her. "Perfection is ours to behold, ours to hold."

She closed her eyes against the great sprays of water now pelting her face. Honorius wished he could rush forward to spread her pale legs in front of everyone and take her there, wet, wild, unrelenting, but he forced himself into a statue pose, for he must play his role, he must be heroic Perseus to her Andromeda enchained.

He threw back his head and began to recite his beloved Ovid: "Chained to a rock she stood!
Young Perseus stayed his rapid flight,
To view the beauteous maid.
So sweet her frame, so exquisitely fine,
She seemed a statue by a hand divine,
Had not the wind her waving tresses showed,
And down her cheeks the melting sorrows flowed.
Her faultless form the hero's bosom fires;
The more he looks, the more he still admires . . .
The beauteous bride moves on, now loosed from chains,
The cause, and sweet reward of all the hero's pains."

He rushed across the stage until he reached Britomartis, dramatically breaking her chains with his sword. He swept her into his arms and away from her rocky prison. The drama was nearly over, and he, Perseus, had prevailed.

The audience erupted in applause and shouts of triumph, showering the stage with roses. Honorius grinned, glorying in the adulation.

Then he saw General Sarus out of the corner of his eye, standing just offstage. *Damn him to Hades!* He sighed and placed Britomartis on her feet. Picking up a rose, Honorius bowed to the audience, then walked over to Sarus.

He breathed in the flower's sweet scent. "What is it now, General?"

"*Venerabilis*, forgive the intrusion, but I have important news of Rome."

The rose fell from Honorius's fingers. An icy-cold surge tore through his gut, for Rome, his dear, sweet bird, had not been eating, and he feared she had taken ill. "Wh—what happened to her?" he croaked.

Suddenly, there was thunderous applause, and Honorius glanced at the finale, a mock sea battle raging across the stage. He felt faint. Tears filled his eyes.

"The siege is lifted, O Great Emperor Honorius. King Alaric . . . "

Honorius could barely hear General Sarus. *Alaric? What has Alaric got to do with my beautiful Rome?*

He tried to listen, but the noise was still too great. Finally, Sarus leaned in, saying into his ear, "Alaric has taken the treasure. The siege of Rome has been lifted, and, my lord, there is other news—"

This last was drowned out by laughter and shouts, but Honorius cared not. Giddy with relief, he wiped his eyes. Rome was alive! He pushed past General Sarus and started for his chambers, for he wished to hold his chicken, his pretty, pretty bird.

"Honorius, *Serenissimus*, please, you must listen to me. Do you not wish to hear what I've learned about the traitor Magnus and his bride, the flute-playing whore?"

Startled, Honorius spun on his heel. "What? The bitch Gigiperrin has been found? They're married?"

The general nodded and opened his mouth to speak, but the uproar in the theater was now insufferable. Frowning, Honorius crooked his finger at Sarus and then led him toward the royal apartments.

*

Honorius stroked Rome, who clucked at him in joy. His heart was full as he fed her little tidbits of apple, her favorite food.

General Sarus cleared his throat. "My lord, Constantinople may yet send reinforcements, but I fear we must give in to Alaric for now, in case—"

Honorius waved him off. "We shall handle Constantinople. You must arrange a meeting with the Visigoth king. Although it greatly pains us, we'll have to give in to Alaric the Uncouth, but Sarus," he stared hard at the general, "you make certain Magnus is killed as soon as possible. We would prefer you use a poison that causes a lingering, painful death, but a swift knife to the gut would do the job just as well. Whatever the case, make sure he suffers. Then find Gigiperrin and bring her here, for we have some unfinished business with her."

Sarus bowed and moved off, not turning his back to Honorius until he reached the door.

Honorius lovingly touched Rome's feathers, for in her he had the world, he had everything he desired.

Except . . .

He saw Gigiperrin again. Her lips in a fulsome pout. Her green eyes sparkling with tears. Her breasts high and heaving in fear.

He grew hard and glanced at Rome, then called for Britomartis.

Chapter 7

Magnus squinted at the pale winter sun, then glanced away, eyeing the group of fifteen Visigoth noblemen and chieftains who had accompanied him and King Alaric. He pondered how far they had come since the lifting of the siege, some three months past. They had left Rome far behind, and now, as they advanced on Ravenna, Honorius had panicked and agreed to negotiations. With the realization of their goals before them, Alaric's mood was jubilant.

There was not a breath of air as Magnus sat atop his stallion, gazing at the emperor's magnificent royal tent, dyed with bands of red and purple and embroidered with gold. Despite the season, the sun felt warm on his face, and a trace of sweat trickled down his brow. He swallowed, wishing for some beer to quench his parched throat, waiting for some movement from within the tent.

Honorius had spared no expense for this auspicious meeting, rendering the location as opulent and impressive as he could. Even the royal standard had been gilded anew, its top crowned by the requisite golden eagle and the acronym *SPQR*. Magnus snorted to himself. As if "*the Senate and the People of Rome*" actually mattered to that vainglorious ass of an emperor! The standard bore a large, purple flag with an image of Honorius holding the imperial regalia, underscored by the Christian cross. Yet, in the still air, as if bespeaking his impotence before the Visigoths, the flag hung still above the tent, limp, lifeless.

Magnus hid his smile, eyeing the two long rows of axe-wielding guards, who stood at attention outside the entryway. The emperor was no doubt waiting inside the tent, but his refusal to greet them spoke volumes, for Magnus guessed Honorius was probably soiling his gilded throne. Despite the show of wealth and power, Honorius must be aware Rome's preeminence was fading, its future uncertain before the coming barbarian hordes.

A breeze swept in from the north. Magnus closed his eyes, enjoying the sensation of coolness on his brow. When he looked out, he saw the flag unfurl and lift. To his surprise, he noticed something different, something that made his heart race in anger, for another image had been added: Victoria crowning the emperor with a wreath of laurel leaves.

He shook his head and glanced at King Alaric, who looked amused. Aside from the last bit of audacity, all this grandeur was a foolhardy waste of time and expense, for Alaric hated ostentation. With the exception of greedy Sergeric, it was probably lost on the rest of the Visigoths as well.

The king gave a signal and everyone dismounted. Aside from Athaulf, Sergeric, and Magnus, several of Alaric's other top advisors and military commanders were also part of the delegation. They made a formidable group, rough perhaps, but noble. Magnus stood tall, proud to be counted among them, and prouder yet to serve as their spokesman at the coming reception.

The tent flap opened and the wiry Praetorian Prefect, Jovius, stepped out, flanked by the tall figure of Sergeric's brother, General Sarus, and General Constantius, who stared straight ahead and didn't make eye contact. Magnus frowned. Even from this distance, the ill-disguised sneer on Sarus's face was plain to see.

Magnus stepped forward and said pointedly, "Jovius, Constantius, well met."

"Quintus Pontius Flavus," Sarus responded, tilting his head and smiling scornfully, "we had thought you dead."

Unflinching, Magnus didn't even glance at him. The man's effort at a slight, by dropping the use of his honorific name and senatorial rank, was not worthy of his time.

"Jovius, King Alaric of the Visigoths stands prepared to receive the titles and lands as requested and which are due him," Magnus

ever achieve the homeland and respect they deserved.

They rode hard for over a mile, until Alaric slowed to a walk and the others followed suit.

"Magnus," Alaric motioned to him, "ride beside me. Athaulf, you, too."

When the three were riding abreast, Alaric shook his head, frowning. "I was wrong to explode as I did," he admitted. "The things Jovius said in Honorius's name, and reading such demeaning tripe in front of everyone, I could have torn both their throats out! I was justified in what I said, but I know well enough our future homeland must, *must* weigh more heavily than pride, and for that I am sorry."

"Do you wish me to go back?" Magnus asked dubiously. "I would suggest waiting a few days. I'm sure they are every bit as angry with you as you are with them, especially since your words actually held more than a little truth in them."

"Perhaps we need to ask for less," Athaulf suggested. "Forget the title for now. If we can get some agreement, some amount of land for our people, that will give us time, and then perhaps we may add more in the months and years to follow."

"Give Honorius a week to cool off," Magnus offered. "He will be getting new reports from the northern provinces soon, and he may yet come to realize how badly he needs you on his side. Then we can send a request for another meeting. We might ask if he has a counter-proposal he is willing to put forth."

Alaric nodded. "What is the least land we can tolerate? Noricum and Dalmatia? Noricum alone?"

Athaulf shrugged. "Noricum would do for now—"

The sound of drumming hoof beats broke through their conversation, and the small group reined in, alert.

A Visigoth horseman cleared a rise in front of them at full gallop, and then wrenched his lathered horse to a halt. His eyes were wild and his leather breastplate slashed and bloody.

"King Alaric, hurry! Queen Verica sent me—we've come under

attack—Roman troops—they ambushed our people while you parleyed—slaughtering women and children! Hurry!"

Gigi!

"Yah!" Magnus shouted and his horse, Agrippa, sprang forward with the others. Galloping toward camp, everyone was jostling for position, trying to find room along the narrow roadway. Three times Sergeric's mount crashed into his, and Magnus had to fight to keep his horse from losing his footing. The fourth time, Sergeric's horse leapt into his, hooves thrashing, as though it were trying to jump over Agrippa, forcing his stallion to stumble violently.

The world spun as Magnus crashed to the ground and rolled, trying to avoid his mount's flailing hooves. He scrambled to get up as the rest of his group galloped away.

O, ye gods, Gigi! He had to reach her, to make certain she was safe, to protect her with his sword. *Victoria, please, I beg you, keep her alive and unharmed!*

Magnus whistled for Agrippa, but the beast was nervous, shying away from him. He heard thundering from behind and quickly drew his sword. Five legionnaires were coming straight at him.

Magnus dodged and swung at the first rider, their swords clashing, brutally jarring his arms. As they turned to face him again, Magnus tried to reach Agrippa, but the horse was too far away. The horsemen charged again and he swung his sword, clipping the nearest rider. A great howl of pain was heard as the man's knee opened up. A blade flashed and Magnus ducked too late, feeling fire in his cheek, blood spraying. He swung once more, then spun, thrusting, opening a gash on the flank of the wounded rider's horse, causing it to scream and rear, before carrying the man away.

Magnus saw an opportunity and dashed for Agrippa, grabbing the reins and mounting in one bound. He charged the nearest rider, but the man got his shield raised in time and fended off the blow. Spinning Agrippa on his haunches, Magnus crashed into two of the horsemen, unseating one. He slashed first right, to ward off a strike, then left—another howl, and this time the rider fell back, his neck open and gushing blood. Magnus pivoted again, ready to attack, but the remaining three hesitated.

Magnus seized upon the opportunity. "Victoria strengthens this arm!" he shouted. He charged the soldier on the ground directly, Agrippa trampling him, then brought his sword up, then down in a great arc, opening the shoulder and chest of the next rider.

Sweat streaked Magnus's face, blinding him. He swiped at his eyes and turned Agrippa toward the last man. He was young and very pale, holding his horse several paces away.

"Will you die with your comrades this day, boy," Magnus asked, "for the sake of your misbegotten emperor? Think on it— he sends you to ambush a solitary statesman, and your friends to murder women and children who have ever been Rome's allies. Is that why you joined the legion?"

The boy-soldier licked his lips, his eyes wide with fright, then he kicked his horse and galloped away.

Magnus! In his mind, he heard Gigi's voice as if from a great distance. Horror gripped his gut, and he raced away, frantic to reach his wife.

*

"Alert!" "Alert!"

Startled, Gigi looked up from tending the fire, hearing shouts and thundering hooves. She saw flames erupt near the far edge of camp and heard screams. Warriors—legionnaires—surged into view, some on horseback, most on foot, slaughtering people she knew, people she loved.

A Roman soldier ran toward her, sword raised, and she grasped a burning branch from the flames, swiping at his face. He ducked and she swung again, striking him across the unprotected skin of his neck. His flesh sizzled and the air reeked of burned pork. Roaring, the Roman lunged and knocked the firebrand from her hand, then stumbled on the rocks ringing the fire pit and dropped face-first onto a jagged edge. His body went still as blood flowed, soaking the ground beneath him.

Gigi ran to her tent. Diving inside, she grabbed for the leather scabbard, which held the dagger Magnus had insisted she wear at all times, cursing herself for not heeding his request. Her flute hung beside the blade in its own leather cover, but she didn't bother to separate the two, flinging both over her head and shoulder.

Panting, she glanced outside. In the distance, she saw two small children lying on the ground and she screamed in defiance. When she got to them, she cried out in agony. Two little girls. Throats slashed. She recognized them as playmates of Berga's. *Oh, God, where is she?*

She heard a great cry rise over the din of battle, and turned to see Randegund drive a spear through a Roman's heart, her silver hair loose and whipping in every direction. She was covered with blood, but Gigi couldn't tell whether it belonged to her or someone else.

Sounds of anguish and terror filled the air. Intent on reaching the children's tent, Gigi dashed down an alleyway, but the swirling smoke was so thick, so dark and acrid, she couldn't see a thing, and stumbled over something. The mutilated body of an elderly man lay grotesquely contorted on the ground, staring out with lifeless eyes. She coughed hard, fighting nausea and the smoke, and then moved on, gagging, groping, feeling her way.

Gigi stopped when she heard some noises—grunts, groans—as horrible as they were familiar. Rage engulfed her, and she thrust her dagger through the wall of the tent, rending it to the ground. Inside, a Roman looked up, startled at the interruption of the rape he was committing on a woman.

Gigi roared her fury, and thrust her blade into his right side, then wrenched up as hard as she could, opening a deep gash. The man simply stared at her in astonishment.

"Bastard!" she spat at him, but his eyes were already blank, and he crumpled to the ground.

Gigi took the woman in her arms. "Laita? Can you talk? You take care of Verica's children, don't you?"

The woman was weeping and incoherent, but there was no time for that.

Desperate, Gigi shook her. "Laita! Where are they? Does the queen have them with her?"

"She . . . I think she has the twins, but Berga and Theodoric are with me," she replied, sobbing.

Gigi frantically looked around. "Where? Where are they?"

"Th—there," Laita pointed to a pile of blankets in the corner.

Gigi raced over and started pulling the covers away. Soon, Theodoric stared up at Gigi, and then Berga's head popped out beside her brother's.

"I could have fought!" Theo told Gigi, his eyes brimming with angry tears.

"No!" Laita hissed. "The Roman would have murdered all of us if we had fought. This way . . . it was my job to protect you—this was the only way you could hope to survive."

"We can talk about it later," Gigi insisted. "We have to get out of here. The soldiers are everywhere, and everything is burning. Grab a blanket—one for each and—hold on." Gigi looked outside and saw little through the roiling black smoke, except a vinegar barrel, a mandatory fire-fighting tool kept within reach of every communal cluster.

Gigi took Laita by the shoulders. "Can I count on you?"

The woman nodded, grim resolve replacing her tears.

"All right," Gigi said. "There's nobody out there right now. Dunk the blankets in the vinegar. Don't ring them out too much, then we'll put them over our heads."

Laita rushed out.

"*Okay*," Gigi said in English, then caught herself. She turned to the children. "It's getting very hard to see and breathe, so we'll go single-file and stay low. Hold on to the person in front of you and cover your mouths. I don't care if the blankets stink, just cover up."

Laita came back with the sodden blankets, and together they draped them over the children and themselves.

"Good. Berga, you hold onto my skirt—tight! Theo, you hold on to Berga's, and Laita, you bring up the rear." Eyes wide with fright, their heads bobbed dutifully. "Nobody let go, not for a moment. Follow me."

Looking outside once more, Gigi listened. The fighting had moved to a different part of camp, but the fires surrounded them. Which was the best way to go? Holding a corner of the soaked blanket over her mouth with one hand, and her knife in the other, Gigi made a decision and started forward.

They crossed the open area and reached the tents on the far side, but the choking blackness made progress almost impossible, except by touch. The wind gusted, and Gigi knew it was the hunger of the flames, sucking in the air around them.

They were all coughing hard, and Berga seemed especially bothered, but her grip was still strong. Good girl! Gigi realized they had to move faster, because her skin was feeling scorched, the fire close, too close. She spun around, dropped to her knees, and screamed over the roar of the inferno. "Berga, get on my back and hold on, tight as you can. Laita, Theo, get down and keep your heads as low as possible."

Scrambling on hands and knees through the caustic, oily, evil darkness, Gigi felt like the smoke was alive, purposefully malevolent, seeking her out, and wanting her dead. Soon, her world was reduced to simply putting one hand in front of the other and moving forward, always forward.

"Jolie!"

It was Theodoric. Gigi looked sideways, and the boy's blackened face loomed close.

"We are past the camp—we should run now!"

Gigi looked around. Indeed, they were in weeds, and the ground had started to rise. She nodded and grabbed his hand, then turned, and looked behind him. "Laita?"

"I don't know where she is," Theodoric said. "We had to let go when we started to crawl, and then, and then she just stopped being there."

Lowering her head in sadness, Gigi knew she couldn't go back for her. She had to get the children to safety. "Come on, run, Theo! Berga, hold on tightly!"

They stood and stumbled up the hill together, and soon the thick, impenetrable dark turned to gray, then suddenly cleared, almost as abruptly as leaving one room and going into another.

Gigi took a deep, sweet breath of frosty air, but her chest seized, and she started coughing again. The kids were hacking, too. She dropped to her knees and looked up. The clear winter sky was indescribably, painfully blue. Her eyes streamed tears as she continued to cough. She glanced around and saw no one else. Were they the only ones to make it to safety?

She looked back at the sprawling camp. Fires blazed in the near ground, and she could still hear the shouts of battle farther away.

"Berga?" Gigi asked when she finally stopped coughing.

The girl shifted on her back, but her grip was still tight. "Where's Mama?"

"She's fighting the Romans," Theodoric piped in.

Gigi studied the hills. "We need to find a place to hide."

"I know a cave," Theodoric said excitedly. "We've played there all week."

Gigi nodded, and together they staggered away.

*

Magnus, where are you? Where are you!

Gigi awoke with a cough and didn't recognize her surroundings in the dim light. She lay back, heart racing, remembering her nightmare. Magnus had been there, just beyond her reach—she could hear his shouts—but she couldn't see him because of the smoke . . .

"Mama," Berga moaned in her sleep.

Attack. Fire. Berga and Theodoric. Memories, horrible memories, came flooding back. Gigi looked around the cave, recalling how the kids had collapsed on the ground after arriving, sick from smoke and fear. She'd joined them there, her mind a blank as to what happened next. How long had they slept?

Her throat felt raw and scratchy as she got up and checked on the kids, snug in their blankets and dead to the world. Magnus and the others had surely returned by now and sent the Romans packing. She thought of Verica, who must be beside herself searching for her children, and knew she needed to get them back immediately.

Emerging from the cave, she squinted at the sun, bright and high in the sky. Oh God, had they slept right through the night? What day was this? Panicked, Gigi ran to a vantage point, looked down on the camp and gaped at the smoldering remains. Had . . . had everyone been killed?

Magnus!

"Oh, no, no," Gigi moaned. She ran down the slope, searching for people, for clues, for him. Everything was burned, in ruins. The smell of smoke clung to the air.

A large mound of freshly dug earth rose from the far side of the devastation. Gigi raced toward it, hoping someone was still nearby, perhaps on the other side. As she got closer, she could see it was surrounded by branches tied together to form crosses, many hung with little trinkets and mementos: a woven bracelet, one of the silken wraps given as payment for the lifting of the siege, a tiny charred sandal. It was a Visigoth grave, a mass burial site. Obviously some had survived to perform this final task for their loved ones, but there was no one here now. In the grass beyond, debris was scattered everywhere, holes remained where tent stakes had been pulled out, and wheel tracks crisscrossed the ground. Gigi followed the ruts for a little while and then looked about. The land was flat, her view unobstructed for several miles. They were gone. The Visigoths had left.

She touched her ring with trembling fingers and looked up at the sky. It was clear, blazing blue, the same shade as Magnus's eyes. *Where are you? Where are you?*

It took her a few moments to gather herself. She had to get the kids up and moving, if they were to have any chance of catching up with the others. Gigi hurried back to the children and roused them from sleep. "Berga, Theo, you have to wake up. We need to talk. Wake up."

They opened their sleepy eyes and gazed at her, then pulled the blankets back up. The soot on their faces made them look clownish, like raccoons with vertical stripes. But Gigi couldn't smile, having a better understanding of what had happened. Yesterday, when they'd first gotten to the cave, she had tried to wipe away the grime on their faces, but it had been futile. After that, they must've slept for fifteen, twenty hours. If anyone had been nearby, searching, the three of them were too far gone to hear or respond.

They didn't know about the cave, she thought in torment. *It was the kids' special, secret place, and now they think we're dead, along with all the others! Magnus thinks I'm dead!* A crushing dread overwhelmed her.

"Children?" She shook them again. "We need to leave now."

*

Gigi warmed her hands, still nervous about the fire, but it was needed. They hadn't seen anyone in days, and the kids were so hungry and cold.

"Here," Theodoric said in a matter-of-fact tone, dumping an armload of bracken, dried moss, and leaves on the ground near the fire pit he'd prepared. "Once I get these bits going better, we can add the branches. I'm sure we have enough now to last the night."

Berga stood wrapped in her blanket and pouted. "I hate fire. I don't want to see a fire ever again."

"But you're freezing. We all are," Gigi said, pulling the little girl onto her lap. "And we need to eat, too, and squirrel doesn't taste good if it's not cooked."

"Squirrel doesn't taste good any time," Berga grumbled and stuck out her lower lip. "Theo should have gotten us a rabbit. I like those."

"Catch your own, then," he shot back. "You don't even know how."

"Enough, both of you," Gigi said. "Theo did a great job today. And when we catch up with your parents, I'm going to tell them how terrific you've both been. Brave, strong, full of good ideas, and if you quit squawking at each other, I won't even mention the grumpy parts."

Theo smiled, then added sticks to the fire. Berga buried her head against Gigi's shoulder.

"I want Mama," she said.

There was the threat of tears in the little girl's voice, and Gigi started to rock the child, watching the flames. *This should be comforting*, she thought. *It's nothing like the inferno.* She looked away, hating her memories, and tried to focus on the days they'd spent together.

Both children had been stoic and tireless. Before leaving the burned-out camp, they'd grabbed what they could from the wreckage, trying to find usable odds and ends. Theo had found coals and a metal tin to keep them in, so they'd be able to carry embers as they traveled. He'd also found an iron pot for cooking, and today he'd rigged a snare, then caught and dressed two squirrels for dinner. After that, he fashioned a tripod to hang the pot over the fire. He was an amazing kid. How many ten-year-olds back home could have done all that? They were brought up differently here, so very differently.

But Berga had found the best treasure of all—two chunks of soap. When they were well away from camp, they'd found a stream and scrubbed their hair and every inch of exposed skin to rid themselves of the oily soot.

Later on, Gigi and Berga dug up edible roots and even managed to find wild garlic and thyme. Everything was in the pot now, and the bubbling squirrel soup smelled wonderful.

Gigi sighed. She had provided little but encouragement this whole time, and wished she could play her flute to cheer everyone up, but she didn't dare. How was she going to do this? Would she be able to hold it together, keep them safe, and travel fast enough to catch up? She figured they were at least a day behind the Visigoths. She hoped they would soon see scouts at the rear, looking for survivors.

And what about Magnus? She could feel his sorrow, his grief reaching across the distance to her. He'd thought he'd lost her once before. Now, since he wasn't here still searching, she knew this time he was certain she was dead. Tears ran down her face, and she put her cheek against Berga's hair, so Theo wouldn't notice.

Don't fall on your sword, Magnus. You promised me! We'll find each other, no matter how long it takes.

Muffled against her blanket, the sound of Berga's tiny voice drew Gigi's attention away from her pain:

Atta unsar thu in Himinam weihnai namo thein,
Qumai thiudinassus theins wairthai wilja theins
Swe in Himina jah ana airthai . . .
Our Father, Who art in Heaven . . .
Berga was praying. Gigi's tears fell unchecked.

Chapter 8

"I refuse to believe you are dead, Gigi. By the gods, it is not possible."

Anguish prevailed, the emptiness in Magnus's heart so deep and black he feared he could not abide by her wishes—he must escape this agony and join her. But no! He could not! On his wedding day, he had sworn an oath to Gigi that he must never kill himself, as he had been trained to do as a Roman military commander, as he was expected to do if he suffered loss or defeat. He had kissed Victoria's image on the ring and vowed to choose life, no matter how dark things seemed, for Gigi had told him in living there was hope, still hope, and he must honor her by doing just that.

He stood alone on the mountainous crags facing north, imagining he could see beyond the mists, to the place where he last held his beloved wife.

Yet now—*O, ye gods*—now, their tent was a smoldering wreck, perhaps her body, too, like so many others, burned beyond recognition, lost among the charred remains in the burial pit, gone, gone.

He gripped the silver ring she had given him, fell to his knees, and kissed the band. "Oh, my sweet," he whispered, "where are you? I cannot believe the gods would be so cruel. Victoria, give me a sign."

Tasting his tears, he remembered the first time he saw Gigi at the baptistery in Ravenna, when the air seemed to sparkle with briny splendor, when she appeared from the mists of time.

Magnus touched his chest, fingering the locket with Gigi's hair and then he flinched, hearing the soft *swish* of parting grass.

He held his breath and listened, perceiving light footsteps on the path, the barest of sounds.

He let out his breath slowly, then reached for his sword.

*

Randegund crept forward. She felt a bitter wrath watching the despicable Roman holding his sword. Suicide was too easy. He must be made to endure all the torments of the world like her Verica, who was wasting away, inconsolable over the loss of her children.

"Magnus!" she shouted.

He turned, eyes widening as he beheld her face. But his gaze dulled quickly, his features the image of suffering.

She drew herself up. "Do not kill yourself, fool, else you will never find your wife."

Randegund waited. He was still filled with pain, but truly— there it was, a look of confusion. She had his attention.

"She is alive, Roman. I saw her. She ran from your tent, knife in hand. But I fear—"

He roared to life, leaping from the crags, running at her, grabbing her. "Why have you said nothing of this? Where is she, Witch of Rocesthes? Tell me!"

She felt shaken to hear her old name, the one used when she was young and vital, when she rode with the warriors, when she was truly *alive*.

Magnus pulled her close, until they were nose to nose. "Where is my wife?" he growled.

Cursed Roman! His strength shocked her, her body withering beneath his might. He had her under his power, and she knew she must regain control. Yet still, she could not find her voice, suddenly fearing he would hurl her against the rocks.

Randegund took a deep breath, then another, finally whimpering, "Release me! Do you wish to find her? Let me go!"

She looked into his eyes and saw his pupils, dark pinpricks, his hatred bared, but there was something else there, a spark of hope. It was no consolation that she should give him such a gift, however false, but it would buy her time. Her thoughts raced, scrambling for something to say. But what? What could she tell him?

And then she recalled a tale of old, and in it she found her answer. Send him away on an unending quest like Odysseus, keeping his hope alive, eternal, only to be dashed again and again, his suffering equal to his hope, and both without end.

She glared at Magnus as she shook herself free. "She was taken by the Romans as a slave. I saw her carried away on horseback. Someone said she would fetch a great price in Constantinople."

Even in his hope he looked shattered, and she gloated in victory. He stared into her eyes, searching for the truth in her words, then turned his back on her and raced down the hill.

She looked up at the sky, thanking the gods for the gift of vengeance.

*

It was nearly sundown. Alaric had watched Magnus ride away from camp earlier that day, heading east, and still he was troubled by the whole situation.

"I do not trust my mother," Athaulf said from over his shoulder. "Why did she not bother to tell us about Jolie, er, Gigi's fate before this?"

Alaric felt uneasy. Athaulf had put voice to the very crux of his concerns, and deep within he agreed with his brother-in-law's disquiet. He feared Randegund's hatred for the Roman had finally steered her soul toward the dark pit of damnation and eternal hellfire.

He had to find her, to question her, for he knew a way to guarantee she was telling the truth, the only way.

Alaric walked away and was relieved when Athaulf did not follow. He spotted Randegund by the campfire, stirring something in a pot.

"Mother," he called out, "we must talk."

He saw the way she looked askance, as if seeking escape. His heart felt cold as he reached her side and noticed her face was already a mask of calm.

"Mother, come."

He walked slowly, leading her away from camp, well past the last posts of his sentries. The men started to follow, but he bade them stay, for he needed privacy.

Alaric halted by the river. Randegund had fallen several paces behind, and he waited for her to reach his side.

"There shall be a full moon tonight, a blue moon," she said, staring at the eastern horizon.

He ignored her flight of fancy. "I shall ask this but once, Mother. Did you tell Magnus the truth? Was his wife taken by the Romans, to be sold in the slave markets of Constantinople?"

She turned to him. Alaric studied her pale eyes, which reflected the violet cast of the sky. He saw for the first time a rheumy trace, the harbinger of old age.

"Mother, answer me," he deliberately made his voice a shade gentler, "and swear you told the truth. Swear it—on my life."

Randegund's gaze did not waver. "My son," she said, "on your life, I do swear I saw her alive, although I cannot say what happened to her once she was out of my sight."

He frowned and she walked away.

Alaric realized his fists were tightly clenched, and he purposely flexed his hands. Once more, he looked toward the east, but Magnus had long since vanished on his quest, lost in the distance, and doomed to failure.

He stood for a time alone, watching the coming night, until the moon rose cold and blue, a witch's moon.

*

Shaking with fatigue and relief, Gigi grasped the children's hands as they made the last, weary ascent up the Palatine Hill. Their clothing was filthy, stiff with their sweat. By her count it was nearly a month since the Roman soldiers had ambushed the camp, a month since they'd been left behind to find their way alone, unaided, to the only refuge she could think of after they'd lost all trace of the Visigoths: Placidia.

Gigi kept her gaze on the ground. The people of Rome stared openly, even malevolently at them—barbarian beggars. It was mid-spring and the weather was growing pleasant, the days longer. The siege had been lifted only four months earlier, and Rome was still, understandably, seething with hatred for the Visigoths. But they kept their anger in their eyes, letting a bedraggled woman and children pass without persecution.

Arriving at the palace gates, Gigi forced herself to stand tall and speak with determination. "I must see the princess," she told one of the guards. "Call the steward Leontius. Tell him I am the one who bears the ring of Quintus Pontius Flavus Magnus, Senator of Rome, so that he may vouch for my identity."

The gatekeeper's expression passed from condescension, through indignation to uncertainty as she spoke, and he hurried off when she finished. Moments later, Leontius came forward, his eyes lighting up as he drew near.

"Open the gates!" he ordered the guards as he hustled to greet Gigi and the children, escorting them inside. "I will be but a moment," he said as he rushed off to find Placidia.

Waiting in the audience chamber of the grand palace, the kids clung to her, terrified by their majestic surroundings. Berga buried her face in Gigi's skirt, hugging her as if she'd never let go.

"Look," Gigi said, seeking to distract them, "if you look at the pretty floor, you will see your reflection."

Theodoric hazarded a glance at the highly polished green marble, then gaped. "Berga, look," he said. "See that? It's better than any mirror!"

The little girl peeked out and stared. "I look dirty," she said with a pout.

"Gigi!" Placidia cried, her footsteps echoing as she ran toward them, her arms outstretched, Elpidia following close behind.

The princess enveloped Gigi in her arms. "How—why are you here? Oh, I have worried you were dead—what—who are these little ones? Where is Magnus? Tell me, you must tell me everything."

"Placidia," Gigi responded. "Please, can the children have something to eat first? Some soup or porridge? We haven't had much, and they have been very brave, but they're suffering."

"Right away, and baths afterward," Elpidia said, and rushed off toward the kitchens.

Placidia crouched down, eye to eye with the children, and took their hands. "My name is Placidia. I have met some of your leaders and hold your people in great esteem. What are your names?"

"This is Theodoric and Berga, prince and princess of the Visigoths," Gigi responded quietly. "They are King Alaric and Queen Verica's children."

Placidia gazed up at her, mouth open. "Why are they with you? What has happened?"

"There was a battle at our camp near Ravenna a month ago. I think your bro . . . er, the emperor set up the ambush, because it happened while Magnus and Alaric were meeting with him about a treaty," Gigi said. "The camp was burned out, we escaped, and so did many others, although we don't know who survived, for sure. They left before we could find them. We've come to you because we had nowhere else to go."

"Oh, my dear Gigi, how you and these lovely children have suffered!" The princess took a moment to gather her thoughts, then squeezed the children's hands reassuringly. "We've heard some news of your people within the last week, and I want to reassure you your parents are very much alive and causing the emperor no end of problems." Theo grinned at this, to which Placidia added, "I shall do whatever I can to find them and reunite you. I'll take good care of you until then. You may trust me in that."

The children looked relieved, then gratefully followed Elpidia when she returned with a servant carrying a tray of food.

Placidia rose and stared at Gigi. "Where is Magnus?" she asked, her tone hushed, as if she feared hearing the worst.

"I don't know. I don't know where he is." Gigi's resolve started to crumble, her shoulders to tremble. A huge lump formed in her throat, threatening to burst. "If he's alive—oh, God, I don't even know that much—he surely thinks—they all must think—we died in the fire."

Placidia held her close, letting her cry at last.

*

Standing beside Placidia, Gigi watched Theodoric and Berga idle in the palace's main atrium. Happily sprinkling food into an ornate, marble fishpond, the children were carefree, with no idea why they'd been summoned.

She, on the other hand, trembled with nerves. They had just received news the Visigoths had ridden on Rome, furious over Honorius's ongoing deceit. They'd made a point of not harming the city this time, but they had demanded an audience with Placidia without any of the usual back and forth of envoys, so neither party had any idea what or who awaited them.

Glancing toward the entry, Gigi hoped with all her heart Magnus would be among the delegation. Placidia was silent, her gaze fixed on the doorway, and Gigi knew she was nearly faint at the possibility of seeing Athaulf again.

In an effort to steady herself, Gigi took several deep breaths. It was certain the Visigoths would find unexpected joy today. Would Placidia? Would she?

Leontius entered the atrium and bowed. "They have arrived."

Placidia lifted her chin. "Show them in."

"Children," Gigi called. "Come and stand by me—now—hurry!"

They scrambled to obey, taking her hands, and waiting. Footsteps approached, and Gigi's breathing grew shallow, tears of anticipation pricking at her eyes. "Please," she whispered. "Please—"

"Mama! Papa!" the children suddenly screamed in unison, rushing across the hallway as their parents cried out in disbelief.

Beside her, Placidia remained motionless, breathless, as she and Athaulf gazed at one another. Gigi didn't move, either, not even to brush away her tears.

Magnus wasn't with them.

*

Darkness was falling. Placidia paced the study, clasping and unclasping her hands as Persis and Elpidia hovered nearby, lighting candles.

Frowning, Placidia knew what she was about to do could seal her fate forever, cutting her off from everything she'd ever known. But she didn't care, at least not enough to change her mind.

After the delays brought on by the joyous reunion, King Alaric had pronounced his terms. He declared his control over the Western Empire. He appointed Senator Attalus "Augustus" over Rome. As for Honorius, his status was undecided, and Placidia didn't know whether he would be allowed to rule as a co-emperor, or be deposed. His future, everyone's future, and the fate of the Empire, were now in the king's hands.

Attalus would run everything, with Alaric's direction. Meanwhile, Alaric had taken the title of *magister militum*, something he'd sought ever since Stilicho's death, and there was also talk of land grants. But, for now, Rome's grain supply in Africa had to be secured for the new government. The Visigoths would still have to wait for their land.

And Magnus—such horror! After the briefest moment of relief at the news of his survival, Gigi was devastated by the tales that had sent him abroad on a fruitless quest. Placidia knew she was heartsick, knew she should go to her friend, but she was compelled, for the moment, to follow another path.

Standing near the door, one eyebrow cocked in disapproval, Elpidia cleared her throat and opened the door to Athaulf when he arrived. She bowed and left the room, dragging a staring Persis with her.

He was here at last! Placidia swallowed, then gazed at Athaulf for several moments. Standing in his presence, she was amazed anew, for he was the embodiment of male beauty, his features sheer perfection, his stance noble, his shoulders broad. And his eyes! They were mesmerizing, flickering golden brown, then green, dazzling in the candlelight.

Athaulf dipped his head, very formal. "Princess, you requested my presence?"

Placidia's heart pounded, and she found it hard to speak. "You . . . Athaulf, you brought us food. I knew it was you from the first, because of the, the . . . your scent was on the satchel."

He looked taken aback, unmasked as he was.

"Tell me," she asked, breathless, trying to focus and remain calm, "why did you endanger yourself for . . . for us?"

"I did it for you alone, Placidia."

She stood without responding, his beautiful eyes boring into hers, and she longed to rush into his arms.

"I couldn't bear to think you were suffering," he added. His hand moved slightly, and for the first time, Placidia noticed he held a silk bag. "I return this to you with the gratitude of a people and with my heartfelt thanks."

Placidia approached him, her knees wobbly, her steps slow and uncertain. She felt small and vulnerable when she finally reached his side, for he was almost a head taller than she.

He pressed the bag into her hand, then stood back. "We shall never forget your generosity, but this is yours, must always be yours. You wore it when first we met."

She smiled, feeling the weight of emeralds and gold, her necklace returned, the gesture so touching. "Thank you," she said, then impulsively added, "I owe you my life, and I would bestow a kiss of gratitude upon you, but you must kneel, for I cannot reach so high."

Athaulf went down on one knee, still keeping to protocol, and Placidia breathed in his scent. Leather. Lavender. She leaned in and touched her lips to his right cheek. Closing her eyes, she lingered against the warmth of his skin, then moved back slightly to kiss his other cheek, but her will gave way to desire and she brushed her lips against his instead.

"Athaulf," she whispered.

He returned her gentle kisses, his fingers touching her arms in a light caress. The heat of him sent a pulse of desire straight to her core.

"Take me in your arms, Athaulf."

She felt his hands at her waist, drawing her down, and she moaned as he grasped her to him, as his mouth covered hers. She wrapped her arms around him. The sensations were overwhelming, and she pressed her body against his, feeling his desire, willing him to keep going, to demand more.

"Placidia," he held her face and stared at her, his breathing heavy.

"Take me with you," she pleaded, looking into his wonderful eyes. "Take me away from here, take me . . . take me—"

"Don't speak like that! You don't know what you're asking," Athaulf said, his voice ragged and low. "You are a princess of Rome."

"Then you don't feel as I do?" Placidia asked, desperate, searching his expression for an answer. "I was so certain you loved me."

"Of course you have my heart, but it is impossible what you ask. Impossible," he said wretchedly, holding her close. "You would be hunted mercilessly for having abandoned the Empire in such a manner. And I could never impose exile on you. It is too harsh, too bitter to live without a homeland, condemned to wandering."

"You are all the homeland I will ever need, Athaulf. I know it. I can't breathe without thinking of you, day and night, every night . . . all night." Placidia reached up and touched his cheek, then kissed him again. "If you can't take me with you, then stay tonight at least, make love to me . . . Athaulf, please . . . we will make a bond, seal our love forever."

"Stop, Placidia! Say no more. I love you too much to inflict such a fate upon you."

"But it is a fate of my own choosing," she insisted, trying to kiss him again, but he tilted his head away. "Athaulf, don't fight this. Make love to me."

"No, you do not understand. You are a maid—"

"I am fully aware—"

"No! I swear if I so much as kiss you again, I will take you here, now, on the floor, and it would be no fitting thing for a princess, I assure you!"

The brutality of his words stunned, but also stirred her, and she imagined feeling the weight of him upon her and yearned for the act.

"Athaulf . . ."

"Placidia, do not ask more of me than I can bear. You would hate me for it afterward."

Crushed and ashamed, Placidia turned her face away. She'd made her bid, uttered words, begged him. She had admitted to feelings she thought could never be possible for her, yet he'd refused, placing honor above all else.

"Politics dog our every move, whether we would have it so or not," he said, his voice still ragged, but calmer. "We are each pawns in this game."

"Go."

"Placidia!"

She pulled away from his grasp, rose, and walked to a table, her back turned so she could not see his beautiful eyes any longer, so he could not see her tears.

She squared her shoulders. "That is all. *Vale*, Athaulf."

There was a moment of hesitation, then she heard his footsteps receding, and the click of the door as it closed behind him.

Placidia gazed at the silken bag, proof he had thought of her, too, day after day, night after night, over these many long months of separation. He loved her, yet he'd refused her utterly.

She dropped to her knees and opened the bag. Her necklace slid out, glittering with the same green fire she'd seen in Athaulf's eyes.

Placidia put her hands over her face and sobbed.

PART TWO

Chapter 9

Magnus stood on the great wall of Constantinople, looking out over the Golden Horn. Cloaked in purple, the boy-emperor Theodosius and his older sister, Aelia Pulcheria, were just visible in the distance, faint shapes on the prow of the royal galley as it rowed up the great bay. The day was fair and windy, yet the Horn was smooth as glass, its protected waters mirroring the blue of the sky with its tracery of clouds.

Tall for his age, the young emperor of the East was near to manhood and therefore desirous of finding his future empress. The coming ceremony made Magnus's heart quake, his whole body shudder, as he stood with a contingent of nobles, waiting for the docking of Theodosius's ship. Would Gigi be led to the parade grounds among the horde of candidate brides? Would he see her soon? Was it possible?

Magnus had searched far and wide these many months, riding the length and breadth of the eastern territories with nothing but rumor to go on, and the conviction Gigi was alive out there, somewhere, for the moment beyond his reach—but alive. When he'd heard Theodosius was about to choose from among the most comely unmarried women in the land, he'd rushed back to Constantinople, hoping and praying Gigi would be included in the procession of beauties.

He knew it did not matter if the girl were a slave or peasant, or even if she were over a decade older than Theodosius. Candidates were chosen not by rank or age, nor by family wealth or title, but for beauty alone, specific requirements regarding perfection of face and form, measurements of bust, waist, and feet a must.

And Gigi was truly a vision for all ages. Magnus shut his eyes, seeing her golden-haired beauty, his thoughts a jumble of contradictions both good and ill: if she were here, it would mean he had found her at last; yet if she were among those selected, Theodosius might seize upon her looks, choosing her above the rest.

"Nephew, they are being led forward. Is she among them?"

Magnus shielded his face against the bright sunshine. He strained to see past the troops drawn up to meet the royal galley: two sets of imperial guards, the *scholarii* in red tunics and bearing long swords, and just beyond, the *hetairia*, their gilded shields glittering in the sun like a spray of stars. He looked past them to the imperial contingent that accompanied the emperor and his sister on the galley—oiled and bejeweled courtiers, bald eunuchs, gray-bearded advisors—and then focused farther on, studying the cluster of women and girls. Varying degrees of prettiness greeted his eyes, but none of them could match Gigi in sheer beauty or grace.

Sweet Gigi.

He swallowed and fought back his emotions, then tried to see all the way down the line of women, but he could not distinguish much from this distance. They were too far away, too blasted far.

"I must get closer, Uncle," Magnus said tersely.

Britannicus nodded. He was his father's youngest brother, a great war hero, who closely resembled Magnus in looks.

"Nephew," Britannicus warned, "do not get too near, or tarry by the women. If someone dares question you, just pretend you are me and leave quickly. If Gigi is there, I will take care of it later."

Magnus smiled. Britannicus was an influential man at court, married as he was to the first cousin of Emperor Theodosius's mother.

Of all the members of his family, Magnus realized he was now deemed the only failure. He had no real place in Constantinople any more—and he was considered a traitor in the west—his existence now utterly dependent on the charity and forbearance of his powerful kin.

But it did not matter. Nothing did. Not if he found Gigi.
He set off for the nearest stairwell.

*

Inching forward, Magnus took care not to step on toes as he moved toward the forefront of the crowd. Theodosius had disembarked from his galley only moments before. His personal Guards of the Purple, his flaxen-haired *Germani* thugs, held their great axes before them, forming a formidable knot around the smiling boy-emperor and his elegant sister.

There was an apple in Theodosius's hand. Like Paris, Prince of Troy, it would be given to the woman of his choice. Magnus's gaze flew down the line, scanning the aspirants' features; coal-black curls framed a winsome face, followed by a blur of other girls and women, all beautiful brunettes and redheads, another girl with raven-dark hair, and then, and then . . .

A young woman stood near the middle of the line, her figure slight, almost too slender, yet proud, her blond tresses barely visible beneath a gossamer veil of green silk.

Magnus willed her to turn. *Look at me!* he wanted to shout. *Look here! Let me see your face!*

He waited, hoping, praying to the gods for mercy at last.

To his horror, Theodosius stopped before her, Pulcheria at his elbow. The crowd grew silent, expectant.

"Alas, it was through a woman that evil entered the world," the young emperor said, smiling at the blonde. He raised his hand, hefting the apple for effect, then glanced at his sister, her face calm, a vision of neutrality. "And," Theodosius went on, "it is said Eve—."

"My lord," the blond girl interrupted, "it is also through a woman that One who is greater than evil entered the world, for a young woman, the Virgin, gave birth to Jesus Christ."

Gasps erupted from the crowd, and Theodosius's mouth dropped open, while Princess Pulcheria flushed red as the apple.

Magnus shook his head in wonder, for here was a girl who certainly had Gigi's spirit, someone with enough daring to challenge an emperor. Although this girl's voice was not nearly as strong, there was something familiar, a spirited timbre, which caused him to take a step forward in hope his memory had somehow dimmed, that it was really she.

One of the guards turned and looked directly into Magnus's eyes, then raised his axe ever so slightly.

Magnus fell back, disappearing into the chattering crowd, and took another position, one less conspicuous, but nearer the girl. Meanwhile, Theodosius had strolled on, still searching for his bride. Magnus guessed he would choose a shy one now, for it was clear his brush with the bold girl in green had thoroughly rattled him.

Suddenly, she turned and stared in Magnus's direction, as if to challenge the yammering crowd, as if to say, *I am not ashamed.*

He sighed. Her eyes were as beautiful as Gigi's, sparkling with life, but they were blue as the sky, not green, not green.

O, ye gods! Why have you forsaken me? Magnus sadly thought. *Victoria, where are you? Where is my wife?*

"Gigi, will I ever find you?" he whispered to no one. Listlessly, he glanced at Theodosius and saw Pulcheria take his arm. She directed him toward another group of several young women, dressed alike in silver gowns.

Someone in the crowd called out, "The emperor now considers the princess's ladies-in-waiting," just as Theodosius stopped. He suddenly grinned, then handed his apple to a beautiful girl, a slim blonde with big eyes and a gracious smile.

So, he had found the one. Grim, bitter, Magnus turned away, determined to drown his sorrows, and ran straight into his uncle.

"She is not here?" Britannicus asked the question, but clearly he already knew the answer. "I am sorry. Come," he added, placing his arm around Magnus's shoulder. "Your aunt awaits us."

"Forgive me, Uncle, but I would dine alone this night."

Britannicus frowned. "No, this is not a night to dine alone, dwelling on dark thoughts. You need your family. Come home with me."

Magnus shrugged. "As you wish." But he had no intention of staying overlong at his uncle's house, not on this night, perhaps not ever again.

*

Magnus awakened from a dream of the olden days, of golden places and distant times. He could not stop thinking of his grandmother. He closed his eyes again, willing himself to sleep some more. He drifted off a little, seeing her again, her hair pure white, her eyes warm and brown. He was twelve when she died, but he always remembered how she looked at him one moment during her final year, how her gaze went to his face and lingered. He could not comprehend why her eyes welled, but later his father told him the reason; she felt as if she were young again and staring into the face of his paternal grandfather, the love of her life, whom she had first met during childhood.

Love. It was powerful—uplifting, poignant, and powerful, so powerful. An image of Gigi rose in his mind, and Magnus smiled. *My sweet, my dearest wife.*

He rolled over and opened his eyes, not fully comprehending, for a stranger lay there, not a finger's width away, someone coarse and bloated, ugly. Her blond wig was askew, her lips painted, smeared, and much too red. What in Hades was he doing here? How long had he—where was Gigi?

He shook his head, addle-brained from too much cheap wine, from months of drunkenness. The room spun, and he groaned in pain, his head splitting. The whore opened her eyes and belched. Her breath smelled of vomit.

"Do you want another taste of this?" she asked, spreading her legs. "Half price."

Repulsed, he bolted from the bed, ignoring his pain, and then scrounged in his clothes for a coin. When he found one, he tossed it without looking, not caring what it was worth. "No," he said, dressing on the run. "No, no!"

He raced for the door.

*

"May the gods pity me!"

Magnus wept, not trying to hide his tears from the passengers and crew of the galley. *Where is Agrippa?* he wondered for the hundredth time. *What have I done to my horse?*

He couldn't recall. Had he sold him while in one of his drunken stupors? Was that what happened?

May the gods have mercy upon my noble steed. Victoria, keep him safe from harm. I beseech thee!

Wiping his eyes, Magnus looked out at the receding walls surrounding the Harbor of Eleutherius, the great city of Constantinople fast fading into the mists. Oars moved in their oarlocks, lapping in the Sea of Marmara, soft, echoing sounds.

Magnus turned to face the west and gripped the ship's handrail. Only one person could help him now, only one.

Placidia.

Chapter 10

Rome. It was all he could think about. What was left of his life, of normal, of good and decent, resided there. Magnus was determined, if he had to live, that his remaining time on Earth would not be wasted in fruitless politics or endless searching, but given to one who was worthy of honor, his friend, that good and noble lady, Placidia.

But he was weary. Weary of walking along the Via Salaria, weary of dust and grime. The vermin that had taken up residence on his body nearly drove him mad, and his need for drink was worse. *Soon*, he thought. *Soon I shall be clean, have a bed and decent clothes, and wine, fine wine to slake my thirst. Rome is not too distant, not any more.*

Magnus passed a milestone, but he did not need to check the distance to Rome's Forum. He knew he was close, so very near, but coming over the crest of a hillock, a scene met his eyes he hadn't expected.

Tents covered in crimson hides, banners boldly displayed, the smoke of hundreds of individual campfires filled his view. The Visigoths.

"By the gods," he muttered, "they have done it again." Another siege. *How dare they!* Angry, he decided to begin his service to Placidia there and then.

Sentries shouted his name as he passed, but Magnus waved them off as he stomped past row after row of tents. He moved with a single-minded determination, ignoring the others who called out, until he reached the king's tent.

He threw open the flap. "Alaric!" he yelled. But when his eyes adjusted he saw only Randegund. "Bitch!" he said, then paused, noting how she cowered. He'd never seen her cower, not in battle, not before men, never, so why . . . ?

He let the thought pass, for she wasn't worth his trouble. "Where are your sons?" he demanded.

Her eyes were wide with fear, her voice barely audible. "Hunting, until dusk."

It was mid-August. Dusk wouldn't come until well into the evening, and it was barely past midday. "I'll wait," he said flatly. "See that I'm brought food and beer. Lots of both, and be quick about it."

Magnus sat near the fire pit, scratching, grumbling and waiting. Finally, a young woman brought a platter of cold meat, dark bread, and cheese, plus a cup and flagon of beer.

Magnus considered the fare hungrily, then smiled. "I have a long wait ahead of me, child. Roll out the barrel so I can serve myself, then be on your way. I'll have no more need of you."

"As you will, my lord," she said meekly, and quickly did his bidding.

His hands trembling with anticipation, Magnus grabbed the flagon and sloshed drink into the cup, then emptied it in one, long swill. Little rivulets ran down each side of his mouth, but he didn't bother to swipe at them as he poured himself another, and then a third.

*

Stunned, Alaric stood over the inert, nearly unrecognizable body, and then looked at Athaulf and Verica. "And you say Magnus arrived on foot?"

"There is no sign of his horse," Athaulf muttered. "What shall we do with him?"

"Let him sleep it off right where he is," Verica said. "Give him a blanket and leave the food, but I won't have him inside. He's covered in lice. We can get him cleaned up once he's awake."

"What about Jolie?" Athaulf asked.

"Gigi," Verica reminded him. "She asked us to start using her real name."

"Ah, of course. We must tell him about her at once," Alaric said, bringing the conversation back to what mattered.

"Certainly, wake him up," Athaulf agreed.

"No! He's in no state to know just yet," Verica said. "He would never forgive us if we sent him off in such a decrepit state, filthy and drunk, and he will certainly leave the moment we tell him."

*

Bathed and dressed in fresh clothing, his hangover nearly dissipated, Magnus felt good as he walked back toward the campfire, and smiled as he recalled Verica's scolding, and insistence he get clean. By the height of the sun, he knew it was nearly noon, and he expected Alaric would be joining him for the midday meal.

He recalled how angry he had been when he first reached the Visigoth camp, but now he felt more relaxed, more forgiving. He would question Alaric about his intentions and then help with the diplomatic negotiations, serving as Placidia's go-between.

Without fail, he must serve Placidia.

Alaric, Athaulf, and Verica were all waiting for him. They looked nervous but pleased, and ready to welcome him. Embracing each in turn, he gave Verica an extra hug.

"I'm sorry for how you found me, truly. It won't happen again. You see—"

Alaric raised his hand, cutting him off. "Magnus," he said. "Let's not speak of it."

Magnus bowed his head in acknowledgement. "You must know, old friend, I've no intention of staying here. My place is with Placidia, and it is for her I returned from Constantinople."

"We understand completely." Alaric clapped him on the shoulder and then frowned at Verica. "At least take a few moments to sup with us before you go."

After the king and queen were seated, Magnus took the chair next to Athaulf. Alaric clapped his hands, and three servants appeared. One poured beer into Alaric's gem-encrusted goblet, while another filled drinking horns for everyone else. The third set forth a platter of roasted meat and flatbread.

The servants departed, and Magnus studied the platter. Feeling queasy, the effects of his hangover were resurrected by the smell of food. Tasting his beer, he sought to quiet his churning stomach, but the drink was bitter and not to his liking.

Verica exchanged another long look with Alaric. "Magnus, please, take your ease before us. There is goat and mutton—"

He felt the bile rise in his throat. "No, no, I cannot stay." He glanced around for somewhere to place his horn, then remembered a refusal to drink with them would be seen as an insult. "I've lived with a single purpose long enough—to serve the princess," he took a sip, "but I would ask a hard question, if you don't mind."

Alaric's eyebrows shot up, and he made a gesture toward Athaulf, who nodded and dashed off. "As you wish, Magnus," Alaric said smoothly.

They were behaving strangely, Magnus realized. Was it guilt? And why in Hades had the king sent Athaulf away? "I wonder why you besiege Rome, yet again. More booty? You surely must still have enough to satisfy even a Visigoth appetite."

Alaric glanced at his goblet, then shrugged. "I must fill you in on what has transpired in the past, what, year and a half?"

"But—"

"Magnus, we *must* talk before you depart."

Alaric's deep frown caught Magnus by surprise. He had gotten some news through his family while in Constantinople, but as he listened to the details of what had transpired since the ambush, since the fire, since the day his life ended, he could hardly believe his ears.

There had been another march on Rome that first spring, and Alaric proclaimed Senator Attalus to be the emperor. Alaric and Attalus then moved north and threatened Ravenna. With his back to the sea, Honorius agreed to split but not cede the Western Empire, yet he ultimately reneged when Constantinople sent four thousand troops to his aid. Alaric was forced to retreat to Rome once more, only to find the city on the verge of starvation because the grain supply in Africa was in the hands of Honorius's supporters. Because Attalus refused to attack Africa, Alaric was forced to strip him of all titles and power, and now the Visigoths were back where they had been, at Rome's very gates.

What a debacle! Gazing at the king, Magnus realized he didn't care about any of it. Not anymore. He drained the last of his beer and said, "You will do as you feel you must, I suppose. As for me, I will serve Placidia."

"Uncle Magnus!"

A shock of recognition hit Magnus hard as he jumped up and spun around. "Berga!" He pulled the child close. After hugging him with all her might, Berga squirmed away, and he shook his head in amazement. "She—she survived!"

Smiling self-consciously, Verica nodded. "She did, Magnus, and Theodoric, also. We were so surprised. Blessed God answered all our prayers."

"All?" Magnus searched her face, the familiar pain redoubling as the furies of hope tore at him. "But, have you ever, was there ever any news?"

Verica's eyes filled with tears as she rose and cupped his face in her trembling hands. "Dear Magnus, Gigi is with Placidia, awaiting your return."

Hardly able to breathe, Magnus could only stare at Verica and wonder at the truth in her eyes. "Alive? Here?"

Verica nodded, tears streaming down her face. "Indeed," she whispered. "Indeed."

"Athaulf has brought a horse for you," Alaric said.

Magnus took him in a bear hug, then, rushing headlong, he leapt on the horse and dug in his heels.

The walls of Rome called to him, beckoned, like never before.

*

Magnus arrived at the palace gates and handed off his horse to a guard, just as Leontius hurried into view.

"Magnus!" he declared, his shock plain to see.

Crossing the courtyard at a run, Magnus burst through the doors, scattering terrified servants in his wake. None tried to stop his passage as he ran through the public rooms, opening doors and leaving them ajar as he raced to the next.

"Gigi!" he bellowed. "Gigi!"

He checked more rooms, but all were empty of anyone but servants. *Stop, think,* he finally told himself. *The place is enormous—think—where would she be on a hot afternoon?*

The sounds of a flute drifted to his ears, and suddenly he knew. *Thanks be to all the gods!* Rushing on through the less formal rooms, he made for a particular corridor and out onto the principal balcony overlooking the Tiber River, then he stopped, staring in disbelief.

Placidia was seated, looking out, and Gigi stood beside her, playing her flute, the breeze moving across her gossamer gown, just as it had in so many of his dreams.

It took him a moment to find his voice. "Gigi," he said, sounding gruff to his own ears, a rasp of emotions.

Placidia gasped just as the music faltered, and Gigi lowered her hands slightly, then looked around with a frown.

Magnus took only a single step forward before Gigi was in his arms.

"You didn't—you're alive! Oh, Magnus," she sobbed, "you came back!"

Staggered beyond words, Magnus could only hold her, drink in her honeyed scent and wonder if he were dreaming again . . . but the dreams had never been like this; never had he been able to find her, hold her again, and feel the warmth of her. His unbearable pain started to ease at last, the frost encasing his heart finally melting.

"I had no idea—I thought . . . " he said, kissing her. "Sweet Victoria has delivered me from Hades."

*

Gigi sat on the couch in her room—their room—still dressed in her gauzy amber gown, her bare feet tucked beneath her. She sipped her wine and wondered if the food she'd had delivered while Magnus shaved would be touched before morning.

She felt ill at ease, shy, and was glad for the sense of calm the wine would bring. It had been well over a year, after all, since she'd last seen her husband. She loved him dearly, but it would take time for them to get reacquainted.

Magnus came out wiping his clean-shaven face, with only a towel wrapped around his waist. He'd lost a lot of weight, and his eyes had the same troubled look he had when she first met him. Knowing he'd been through a terrible ordeal, Gigi wondered how she could help him heal. She smiled nervously.

"You are beautiful," he said, leaning against the door. "I can hardly believe you're sitting before me, waiting for me, as you did all this time."

"I never gave up hope. Placidia had her people searching everywhere, but no one could find you. But I had no doubt you'd come back, Magnus," she said, putting her wine down.

With a last swipe of his face, he tossed the cloth on the floor and took her hands. She stood and he kissed the ring on her finger, then her brow. "Victoria watched over me when you could not. I know it."

"We both did what we could." She searched his eyes, trying to convey her feelings, then reached out and touched the thin line of a scar on his cheek. "This is new."

"I got it before the fire, during the ambush. We nearly died that day, you and I."

"But we didn't, and now you're back." Gigi dropped her gaze and nodded toward the wine. "May I pour you a glass?"

Magnus glanced at the amphora and then shook his head. "No. No wine. You are all I need . . . will ever need."

Again, there was a pause, this time more awkward, and their eyes met and held.

Magnus shifted, uncomfortable. "Gigi," he said, "I know it's been a long time. I can't assume . . . "

"Intimacy will come when we're ready. I just need you to hold me."

He took her into his arms and she nestled against him, breathing deeply. Olive oil, hints of pine and spice, new fragrances, but there was more, something she'd dreamt about these long months, the scent of his skin, his essence.

"I am home," he murmured, "at last, I am home."

"Magnus," she whispered back, "I love you."

"It goes far beyond love, my sweet," he said. "You are my life."

They clung one to the other, the ache of their separation still keenly felt, never to be forgotten.

Chapter 11

Sergeric sat on a log near the campfire, close to Alaric's chair. He looked around, confident he was out of earshot of the other chieftains.

"Alaric, have you considered what we discussed at supper?" Sergeric asked.

"I have, but I am not yet convinced."

"I tell you," Sergeric insisted, keeping his voice low, "the Roman woman—Proba—is as sick of this siege as we, and she will command her servants to go to the gate, overpower the guards, and let us in tonight."

"We've been camped outside of Rome barely two weeks," Alaric argued. "Food can't have run short already, not in the summer. I mistrust this woman."

Sergeric shrugged. "You are correct—she is not hungry, except for my cock. She may be rich, of the merchant class, but she has a taste for earthier things. She has come to me many times already, and does not seek our downfall, I can assure you. In fact, she will do just about anything I ask of her. Truth be told, she fears those who tasted human flesh during the first siege far more than she fears us. She worries they will use our presence outside the city as an excuse to revisit their old ways."

Sergeric watched Alaric study the ground between his feet. He waited patiently, guessing it would not take long for the king's response—and certain of the outcome.

Alaric looked up, a familiar glint in his gaze. "We must have firm rules. Sanctuary is to be granted without exception, and no rape or setting the city to flames. The palaces on the Palatine must remain intact, as must the churches. Athaulf will want to go to the princess immediately, I am sure. Also, Magnus and his wife are to be allowed quarter. They are to be left unharmed."

Sergeric smiled and nodded. "Agreed."

He saw a softening in Alaric's expression, the look of trust. That was his weakness, his great failing. The king did not suspect he and Sarus would never forgive him for the deaths of Sarus's wife and children, or for the loss of their father's kingship. They were simply biding their time.

"Good. Send word then," Alaric said, standing, "so our armies will be ready, for this night Rome will belong to the Visigoths."

*

"Mother," Alaric said, entering Randegund's tent, "the decision has been made. Tonight, we will enter Rome."

Randegund bade him sit by her side. "My son," she said as he settled beside her, "this day I consulted the runes, and it is a fortuitous time for our people. You know, even-numbered days bode ill for the Roman scum." She smiled. "But did you also know today is a cursed anniversary for them?"

"What do you mean?"

"Their great mountain, Vesuvius, erupted on this day over three centuries ago, killing many Roman citizens. I think tonight we shall kill many Romans, too."

Alaric was quiet for a moment. "I have given orders to the contrary, Mother."

Ah, Alaric! Ever the noble one. She nodded to him, knowing full well that war was war, however honorable the conquering host, however misguided its ruling king.

*

Getting out of bed, Gigi stood beside Magnus and stretched,

relieved to see him in the warm glow of the oil lamp, sleeping peacefully at last. The first two nights home he could barely close his eyes before violent nightmares would jar him awake, each time leaving him in a cold sweat. He refused to say what they were about, but Gigi guessed well enough.

They had spent most of their time closeted, getting to know one another again, and learning to trust that it wasn't all a dream. Finally, their love overcame any awkwardness, the rekindling of their passion beautiful and complete. Placidia had given them the space they needed, and only insisted they join her for a meal on the third evening, stating with unexpected humor she feared they would die of starvation as they embraced, if she didn't force them to take time out and eat.

Smiling to herself and moving to the balcony, Gigi noticed the odor of wood smoke hung heavier in the hot August night than it usually did at this hour, and she wrinkled her nose, wondering if tomorrow would be another stifling day. She wandered back inside and to their bed.

Magnus was still sleeping, so she snuggled in beside him. His arm closed around her instinctively, and she rested her head on his shoulder, content and happy.

*

Athaulf sat in the dark atop his horse, anticipating the moments ahead. Once inside the Salarian Gate, he would make directly for the Palatine Hill. It would take but a short while to reach it on horseback, and then . . .

He looked up at shouts and the sounds of swordplay erupted from the other side of the ramparts. This was it! Urging his horse forward, he passed King Alaric and gave him a nod. Just then, the screech of surrendering iron told him the Salarian Gate was theirs. With a great swell of war cries, everyone moved forward at once.

But they'd miscalculated—the doors opened outward! There was no room to push them open against the surge. Athaulf shouted orders to back off, but he wasn't heard and the masses of infantry pushed ahead anyway, unaware of the problem, expecting to pour inside.

For a chaotic few moments there was nowhere for anyone to go, until the stress was such that the doors simply broke from their hinges and crashed to the ground. Suddenly, instead of a stealthy entry into the city, there were screams of terror from among their own as many were trampled underfoot.

Athaulf's horse reared in fright, pawing the air, and then tried to bolt, but the mob was too thick around them. Glancing across the masses, he could see Alaric and the other horsemen having much the same difficulty.

Finally, the crush of humanity broke free as many in the vanguard reached the maze of streets beyond the gates and flowed away, but as Athaulf found room to maneuver, great wafts of black smoke billowed across his path.

"Luifs Guth!" Athaulf swore, urging his horse forward as the smoke engulfed them, but it was useless—with everything going on, the animal balked and refused to advance. Dismounting, he tried to find something to cover the horse's eyes, but this was no time of year for extra clothing and there was nothing, nothing!

Jostled by his fellow Visigoths, Athaulf felt a rising panic. This was taking too long. *Placidia!* He had to get to her. Spotting a man with a sack, ready for plunder, he yelled and then wrenched it out of his grasp. Quickly slinging it over his horse's head, he was finally able to make some headway, and soon they passed the worst of it.

Remounting, Athaulf drove his horse on, realizing he had no clear sense of the layout of Rome's winding streets, praying God would guide him to the palace without more delay. He scanned the area, trying to locate the Palatine Hill amidst the darkness and smoke. It was somewhere over . . . *there, there it was!*

"Yah!" His horse leapt forward, and Athaulf did not care as Romans and his own people scattered before them, in fear for their lives.

*

King Alaric urged his horse forward into the smoke, struggling to keep abreast with the surge. This was it, what he had waited for his entire life.

Penetrabis ad Urbem. You will penetrate the city. Randegund's chant echoed in his mind.

A frenzy of shouts roused him, and he looked around. A brazier had been overturned, setting fire to the guardhouse. Nearby, embers and ash wildly blew into elaborate pleasure gardens, the famed Horti Sallustiani, and several large plane trees burst into flames. Hearing panicked screams, he saw Romans fleeing their homes, running in every direction. Alarmed, he searched for some hint of structure in the chaos and spotted a band of Visigoths advancing as a unit toward the Senate building. For the most part, he judged, these men were keeping to orders, but as for the rest . . . ?

Suddenly sensing trouble behind him, Alaric twisted in his saddle.

More fires, hungry flames leapt out of windows and rooftops— *no!* He heard a shriek and spun back to see one of his men raping a young woman right in the street.

"Stop!" he yelled, urging his mount forward and kicking the man with his boot. "Leave her be. You are not to rape!" But the wretch paid him no heed, so Alaric jumped down and pulled the man off his victim, then punched him in the jaw, knocking him senseless. The woman scrambled to her feet, then spit at Alaric and ran away, cursing him and sobbing.

Alaric reached for his reins, but his horse shied and bolted as more Visigoths came on, and he found himself on foot, alone.

Frantically looking around, he realized his army was out of control. With only his authority and his sword to curb the tide, he ran deeper into the city.

Smoke was everywhere, thick and black. Alaric saw three men coming back down the street with sacks of booty, and he was about to continue past, when he noticed one of them carried a lit oil lamp.

"Do not—"

Laughing, the man tossed the lamp against a wall, which burst into flames.

Alaric grabbed the man by the throat, furious. "Your orders were not to burn—pillage only!"

"I take my orders from Sergeric, and he gave us a free hand," he pushed Alaric aside, "to do whatever we please, just as the Romans would do. When in Rome!" The man broke off, laughing again, then sprinted away with his friends, bumping into a terrified woman and causing her to fall.

Dressed in black, her head modestly covered, she was obviously of some religious order. Alaric approached her as thick, acrid smoke filled the air, but she cowered, hiding her face.

"Sister, fear not. I am a friend."

She peered at him, and he was struck by her youth and beauty.

"Sanctuary!" she cried out, whimpering, yet defiant. "I am Marcella, Daughter in Christ, and I claim Holy Sanctuary. But, please, I haven't the strength to get to my church, so I claim it right here, on this spot, before God."

"Sister," Alaric said, reaching out, "I, too, am a Christian, and if you allow me, I will escort you wherever you want to go. I will protect you—I swear."

It took a long time to get the woman to safety, passing bodies, burning buildings, and the horrific din of rape and destruction. After leaving her at St. Peter's, safe and among many of her own, Alaric refused to accept her blessings and grimly continued on.

He moved through the streets, commanding those breaking

his rules to desist, even swinging his blade against some when needed. At other times, he dispatched people in the throes of an agonizing death, and many times, too often, he pulled horrified women from the clutches of their abusers.

What had happened? How had it gotten so badly out of control? He knew Sergeric was partially to blame, but he blamed himself as well. He should have known that once unleashed, a sack would be ungovernable. Lawlessness breeds frenzy breeds every kind of unspeakable evil.

This was his sorrow, his sin to bear. He made the sign of the cross and beseeched God for forgiveness.

*

Dawn approached, the sky lightening despite the heavy smoke in the air. Reaching the Domus Augustana and finding the palace gates broken, Athaulf hastened inside, securing his horse in a side court. He prayed no one would steal him. The palace was supposed to be sacrosanct, yet everything was in turmoil, people fighting, bodies scattered everywhere. *Placidia!* Her soldiers battled the onslaught as best they could. Even servants struggled, almost comically, with pots and pans and broomsticks against his well-armed men.

"Leave the palace at once," Athaulf bellowed as he passed his men. "At once!" He ran from room to room—her study was open and empty—the adjoining imperial bedchambers hacked up, the beds, tables, and couches overturned.

Iésus, where is she? He barged into an unfamiliar room and found one of his own men raping a servant, and he pulled the man's head back and struck him hard with the butt of his sword. "Leave!" he roared. "You're not to touch—"

"Athaulf!"

He spun around to find Magnus, bloodied sword in hand, and

Gigi, looking fierce and holding a club.

"Where is Placidia?" Athaulf cried out.

"Don't know—we haven't found her," Magnus shouted back.

"Keep looking." With that, Athaulf ran off, alarm redoubling over what he might find.

Time dragged as he searched room to room, level by level, yelling at any Visigoths he found, ordering them to leave at once. The place was a labyrinth, and he could only hope, in his despair, that he'd not missed something along the way.

He stopped suddenly—what had he heard? A scream? Athaulf turned and peered behind him, then crept back. There it was again, muffled and indistinct, but very close. Glancing into a room he'd already checked, he considered it more closely, and then caught sight of something he hadn't noticed before, the merest crack of a concealed doorway. He'd seen one like it before at the House of Livia: painted over by botanical scenes and blending with the rest of the wall.

Another sound of anguished struggle, a stifled cry. Athaulf sprinted across the room and thrust open the door.

The Visigoth was half-naked, his buttocks flexed as he pinned Placidia against the wall.

Athaulf's blade pierced the whoreson, jabbing from one side of his waist to the other. The body buckled and fell as Athaulf pulled Placidia into his arms. Bruised about the face, bleeding and naked, she held on to him and wept.

"Placidia, my love, forgive—" His voice strangled. "*Iésus*, forgive me. I tried to get here, truly I did." He held her close and let her cry, tears of his own falling into her hair.

After a moment, her sobbing slowed, and she raised her chin, but wouldn't look him in the eye. "My gown, please," she said, her voice faint but determined.

Athaulf let go and turned away, shoving the dead bastard with his foot to free her things. He handed them to her without glancing back, and she dressed quickly.

"You may turn," she said, her voice ragged with pain.

He faced her. Her gown was bloodstained, and suddenly he was certain he'd arrived too late. Oh, God in Heaven, why had this happened?

Arms folded tightly across her chest, she kept her eyes averted, her agony clear to see. Athaulf held her gently, felt her trembling. "I love you, Placidia. I love you." It was all he could think to say. He had to reassure her he felt no different because . . . because . . .

"We must go see to the others," Placidia said, pushing away from him, her voice a monotone. "I have to protect my people."

"Placidia, I love you. It does not matter if he . . . "

She met his gaze, and he sucked in his breath—her eyes looked dead.

"I thank God you came when you did, Athaulf. He didn't . . . he hadn't . . . not yet."

Then she turned around and left.

*

When Gigi and Magnus reached the atrium, they saw Athaulf standing amid the damaged foliage and broken statues. The place seemed empty now, quiet, the palace abandoned by the Visigoth marauders. They started toward Athaulf, still cautiously looking around, but when Gigi spotted Placidia kneeling on the floor, she rushed forward.

When she reached the princess, she clamped her hand over her mouth. "Oh, no, Placidia!"

Persis was lying in a pool of blood amongst the shards of a broken urn, her skin already yellow and waxy after bleeding to death.

"How dare you, Athaulf, how dare you," Placidia moaned, weeping uncontrollably, reaching out to finger Persis's sodden hair. "You have sent your people to burn my city, rape and murder my citizens, yet you would protect me? I will stand against you,

Visigoth, and fight with my own."

Athaulf bent and touched Placidia's arm, an expression of pain and pleading on his face, but Placidia, covered with blood, suddenly got up and launched herself at him, shoving him backward with all her might. "Stay away from Persis! Don't touch her—this is your doing."

Devastated, he opened his mouth to explain, but Placidia shrieked, "You are no better than any of the others. I will not run away and leave my people to their fate. How dare you suggest such a thing!"

Gigi gripped Placidia by the shoulders, shocked to see how badly battered she appeared. "Who—what happened to you?"

It was only at that moment Placidia seemed to realize Gigi and Magnus were there. Her eyes filled with tears as her face contorted in misery. "Oh, Gigi," she cried. "Persis, my Persis is dead!"

Gigi hugged her. "I'm sorry. Are you hurt?"

Placidia shook her head just as a great gust of black smoke billowed into the room through the roof of the atrium. Shouts followed, rising from nearby corridors.

"We must leave—now," Athaulf warned.

"No," Placidia yelled. "I will not abandon my people!"

"Placidia, we must get out of here," Gigi urged.

Athaulf approached the princess and stretched out his hand.

"Barbarian!" She lunged at him again, but he pivoted and pinned her arms behind her.

"I love you, Placidia," he said, as he scooped her up and carried her outside, ignoring her protests. Athaulf voiced relief that his horse was where he'd left it.

Luck was with them as Magnus spotted another horse nearby, wandering riderless, and within moments all were mounted, the men perched behind the saddles, Gigi and Placidia in them. Athaulf struggled to keep the princess's arms under control and her bottom firmly in place.

As they galloped through the chaotic streets and out of Rome,

Gigi noticed how his face was buried in Placidia's hair, and how he was holding her tenderly against his chest—as a lover would, rather than as her captor.

Chapter 12

After three days of pillaging, the Visigoths left Rome for the countryside, taking their captives with them. Placidia refused to speak with anyone, including Gigi and Magnus, keeping to the traveling wagon provided her during the day and her tent in the evenings. Anguished, Athaulf was convinced he'd destroyed all feelings she had ever held for him, and he tried to console himself with the fact that she was safe, and for now, nearer to him than she had ever been.

Resting after a long day's march, Athaulf sat by the newly dug fire pit, jabbing a stick at the glowing embers. Verica was close by, preparing several pheasants for the evening meal, and Alaric was meeting with men just returned from taking inventory on the booty.

"Athaulf."

He looked up at Alaric, who handed him a horn of beer and sat down.

"The reports are in," he said, "and I must say, I'm surprised and heartened at the plunder of foodstuffs, and at the civility of our people during the attack."

Athaulf snorted and shook his head. "Surely you jest?"

Alaric frowned. "It was a sack and brutal by its very nature, but as far as it went, more men than I would have guessed followed my orders." He spread his hands. "Much burned, but nothing that can't be rebuilt in a year, and true, many died, many were raped, but far, far fewer than I thought—"

"You heard, didn't you," Athaulf cut in, "that the Mausoleum of Augustus and that of Hadrian were pillaged? Our people stole the royal urns, scattering the imperial ashes, as well as those of royal family members."

"And for that travesty, I shall personally apologize to Placidia,"

Alaric said evenly. "But still, it could have been worse, much worse. Above all, the right of Holy Sanctuary at St. Peter's and St. Paul's seems to have been strictly adhered to—"

"And what of the other Catholic basilicas?" Athaulf asked. "Take a good look at our treasure. It is filled with objects from the Roman churches."

"I have seen the loot," Alaric admitted. "Yet many Visigoths did follow my commands. I was not the only one who assisted folks into the basilicas. Lives were saved, many people spared. The bishop of Rome is still alive, as is the princess."

Athaulf frowned. "She was but a moment from being raped when I found her."

"True, brother," Verica broke in, annoyed, "but will your precious princess give us any credit for all the things that went right that day? I think not. Her Magnificence has just insisted dinner be brought to her tent *again*."

Athaulf glared at his sister. "She asks for no more than our mother. Why has Randegund suddenly decided to stay in her tent?"

Alaric and Verica remained close-mouthed on the subject, and Athaulf knew why. They all suspected their mother had blatantly lied to Magnus about Gigi, sending him off on a wild goose chase, either to be rid of him, or more disturbingly, simply to hurt him. Now that he was back, Randegund was keeping well away from all of them. Athaulf shook his head and poked at the coals again.

"She's proving a little bitch, your princess," Verica muttered to him. "Her haughty, willful, pampered self-indulgence is—uh!" she grumbled. "She is much like her brother, conceited and craving flatterers. I can't see why we should go out of our way to accommodate her whims. She should be thankful we were as gentle as we—*Iésus!*" Exasperated, Verica jabbed her knife into the meat, leaving it thus, got up, and marched toward Placidia's tent.

Scrambling to his feet, Athaulf followed and listened from outside the tent as his sister forcefully pointed out Placidia's petty behavior, accusing her of tacitly siding with Honorius by her refusal to stand up to his brutal treatment of the Visigoths over the years.

"*Our* brutal treatment of *you?*" Placidia spat back. "Since we've left Rome, you have ravaged the countryside. What of Campania or Nola or Capua? You targeted the wealthy, despoiling the families, and binding their youth in slavery, forcing them to serve you with their own plate and silver. Is that not brutal? You have no justification to complain!"

Athaulf heard Verica roar in fury. "Realize one thing, you pampered, useless butterfly," she thundered. "Had your depraved brother ordered the sack, no one would have been spared! No woman, neither young nor old, no child, no male. All would have been tortured, raped, debased, and then slaughtered or driven into slavery for his personal lusts. You can't deny it, for that's exactly what he's been doing to my people for years!"

Athaulf stood by as Verica stormed out, but it wasn't until after she was gone that he heard weeping, ragged, bitter weeping. He couldn't help himself, realizing he'd probably be shredded by Placidia's angry nails, but he slipped inside anyway.

Elpidia was there, having made her way out of Rome with Leontius, carrying with them some of Placidia's personal belongings, despite the danger. Hovering protectively near the princess, Elpidia scowled at him, but left the tent, allowing him his moment.

Athaulf knew he had but one final chance, one opportunity to try to make Placidia understand, to bring her back to him. He took her firmly in his arms, partly because he didn't want her to flail at him, but mostly because he wanted to comfort her, and for a time she didn't react.

Then she struggled and tried to push him away, but her arms were caught.

"Placidia," he said, pressing his cheek against the top of her head and rocking her back and forth. "It has nearly killed me to hurt you so badly. Please forgive me. Please. I love you. I want you to love me again, to be my wife. Your anger is destroying me, I swear it."

He tried to kiss her, but she turned her face away, and they stood like that for several moments. Finally, unexpectedly, just as he was about to give up, he felt her shoulders relax, and her hands moved tentatively to his waist. He swallowed hard, relishing the moment, and tightened his grip.

"Verica was right, as much as I hated to hear it," she said, her voice muffled against his chest. "My brother would do—has done far worse, many times. It's just . . . sweet Persis is dead. And Rome, it was mine, my home, my people, my solace, and you hurt her, it, knowingly, willingly."

He sighed heavily. "I know. I'm so sorry."

"Athaulf?"

"My love?"

She looked up at him then, and his heart thudded with hope. Her dark eyes were so beautiful, still sparkling with tears and remnants of anger. He clenched his jaw, wanting to devour her, and it took all of his determination to deny himself a physical reaction to her beauty.

"You wish to marry me?" she asked, her voice barely above a whisper.

"Indeed. Since the first moment I saw you. If you would but give me another chance . . . Placidia, I am yours."

He watched as her eyes traveled over his face, and he recalled the words she'd said, the things she'd asked for, so long ago. Would she ever ask again?

"Tell Verica I must speak with her," she said.

Placidia pulled away then, and he let her go, aching, but hopeful.

*

It was late when Placidia dismissed Elpidia, despite her nurse's pleas to stay. After all, it was time. It was time she stopped being a child, an innocent. Rome was gone and she would never return, could never return. Honorius might think her dead, or he might hear of her escape with the Visigoths. Either way, she didn't care, because that life was over.

Placidia let her gaze roam around the rustic hide tent with its strange adornments: its wooden poles intricately painted with geometric designs, chairs made from interwoven antlers, furs scattered everywhere. She nodded to herself. It was time for her new life to begin.

Verica had helped her dress, brushed out her curls to their full length, and made sure everything was ready, everything but her fear of the precipice from which she was about to leap.

She heard a soft scratching at the tent flap and her heart beat more rapidly.

"Placidia." Athaulf spoke her name softly and she turned to greet him, her throat too dry to respond.

"Verica said you asked for me?" He came inside, but stayed near the doorway. He was wearing a clean tunic and new sandals, Placidia noticed, and she let her eyes wander over him, then blinked and swallowed, forcing her gaze to his face.

He looked as hesitant as she, and then his expression changed to shock. "You—you're wearing the—the gown—from our first meeting!"

Determined, her eyes fixed on his. "True. Verica knew where to find it, since it was a part of the original siege ransom." She held out her hand, her pulse racing, and she wondered if she would faint before . . . before . . .

"Come in."

Athaulf slowly approached, then knelt and kissed her hand, but she withdrew it quickly. "Don't, Athaulf. I'm not a princess any longer. Get up, please."

He smiled at her, his gaze ardent. "I don't kneel for a princess. I kneel to honor the woman I love."

Moved by his words, she reached out and touched his cheek with trembling fingers, then his lips. She had kissed them once passionately, and her mind was filled with the desire to feel their heat again. "Please get up."

Rising, he looked at her steadily, his beautiful eyes soft, warm, and anxious. "You wished to see me?"

She opened her mouth to respond, and then suddenly recalled a conversation she'd had with him once before, when he'd returned her necklace the first time. She blushed deeply, her face hot, her body frozen with discomfiture at the remembrance of that evening, her humiliation after she'd begged him to take her, after he'd honorably declined.

He took her hand again and turned it over, kissing her palm. "You're terrified, like a trapped little bird. Why?"

"Because I love you," she whispered.

He kissed her hair, then her temple, allowing his lips to linger. "And this frightens you, my love? Why?"

Placidia leaned against him, welcoming his gentle touch.

"Tell me, Placidia," he asked as he drew strands of her hair over her shoulder, letting the tendrils run through his fingers, "why are you wearing this gown?"

"Because," she looked up at him, breathing rapidly, "because it is time you returned the necklace to me properly."

She looked to a silk bag on the table, and heard Athaulf stop breathing for the slightest moment, knowing he remembered.

He stepped to the table, opened the bag, and drew forth the emerald necklace. Hands trembling, Athaulf placed it at her throat, and she pulled back her hair so he could work the clasp. When he finished, he hesitated, then bent and kissed her, just above where the necklace lay. "I love you, Placidia."

Sensations, tingling poured over her. "I don't want you to refuse me this time, Athaulf. I want you to . . . stay . . . all night . . . please."

Athaulf took her face in his hands and covered her mouth with his, kissing her with a fervor she had not expected. His tongue sought hers, gently probing, and she let him in. Weak with pleasure, she felt a melting warmth between her legs and moaned with desire.

He suddenly pulled back, concern etched across his face.

"What is it?" she asked.

"You are so young, so . . . I will gladly stay, but if—if you're fearful, after what happened in the palace—"

"No! I mean, I'm not," she insisted, flustered. Clutching him, she said, "There is nothing I want more than to be with you . . . joined with you . . . at last."

Athaulf drew her to him, cradling her in his arms. His lips touched her brow.

She looked up, desperately wanting his kisses, but he was so very tall. Instead, unsure and tentative, she placed her hands against his chest and kissed him there. Hearing his sharp intake of breath, she grew bolder and brushed her lips against him again. The fabric of his tunic was thin, and she could sense his body heat, his rapid breathing. Moving her hands to the small of his back, kissing him still, she reveled in his taut skin and muscular physique. He moaned openly and she closed her eyes, her heart racing as she sensed the roundness of his backside at the edge of her fingertips.

"Athaulf, please."

"What, my love?" His arms tightened and he pressed against her, kissing her hair, and she could feel him, all of him, ready, hard.

"Help me . . . Athaulf . . . my gown."

He fumbled with the straps of her dress, then kissed her hungrily, his desire unleashed as her clothes fell to the floor.

She pulled at his tunic, running her hand over his bare hip, then looked at him and gasped when she saw him fully exposed. She touched him and he groaned her name.

"Athaulf," she said, desperate with longing.

He picked her up, his hands grasping her backside, and she felt the heat of him against her as he laid her on the bed.

"Athaulf!"

This was bliss, perfection, and she cried out as he thrust himself against her. There was a stab of pain and her eyes flew open in shock.

He hesitated. "Have I—"

"No, please . . . don't stop, don't ever stop," she murmured as he started to move gently inside her.

Wanting more, grabbing him, she instinctively forced her hips against his, over and over, and his fever matched her own. She had never imagined so much, never realized . . . and arched as her body exploded with a mysterious, thunderous pleasure, even as Athaulf tightened, and then convulsed, shuddering in his own powerful release.

Her breathing slowed until it matched her heart's deep rhythm, her soul's fulfillment. As Athaulf gradually relaxed against her, she touched her lips to his shoulder. Eyes wide with amazement, she wondered how long it might be before they would do it again, or how anyone could willingly leave the bed, after experiencing such wonders.

Propping himself up on an elbow, Athaulf considered her for a long moment, tracing her cheek, his fingers feather-light as he touched the gems at her throat. "We should take this off," he said, seeking to unclasp her necklace. "I do not want to break it."

She stayed his hands, kissing him over and over, whispering, "No, I am bound by my faith . . . must keep one thing on . . . one thing at least . . . when I am naked before you . . . when we make love."

He smiled and then stroked her breast, and she trembled, yearning for more.

"How long I have dreamt of seeing you like this, of having you so close." His gaze roamed over her body, his desire rekindled. "You are a wonder, a vision." His eyes returned to hers. "I love you, Placidia."

She drank in the nearness of his beautiful eyes, the musky scent of his warm skin. "And I love you," she whispered, touching him. "Please, let's never get dressed."

Athaulf threw back his head and laughed, then kissed her again, and made love to her again and again.

*

The Visigoths moved ever southward into gathering storms. A cold wind howled, the miserable trek made worse when a virulent flu swept through camp.

The rain pattered down as Gigi jumped into bed and pulled the furs up under her chin. She snuggled close to Magnus. "Finally, now it's my time. I thought your meeting with Alaric would never end. Besides, I'm freezing, so do something, but I warn you, I'm keeping every last stitch of clothing on, so you'll have to get creative."

When he didn't respond, she glanced at him in the dim light and saw the look of pain in his eyes; something she'd hoped never to see again.

"What's wrong? You're not getting sick, too, are you?" she asked anxiously.

"No," he replied.

"Then what is it?"

"Nothing."

She stared at him, realizing she'd seen this same expression many times since his return. So far, she hadn't been able to get a word out of him, and she'd always let it pass. Pursing her lips, Gigi decided it had gone on long enough. It was time to force the issue, or at least try.

"What is bothering you, Magnus? Please let me in."

He turned his head away without a word, so she reached up and gently coaxed him back. "You're breaking my heart with this, I swear. Please, what can possibly be causing you so much pain? It's not doing you any good keeping it inside."

Magnus shook his head, his gaze on the ceiling of their tent. "I live with a terrible shame—many, in fact."

"Stop it," Gigi demanded. "You can't talk like that. What can be so bad, so shameful? You spent months looking for me. I don't see the shame in that. It sounds courageous and noble."

"Perhaps it was . . . I was . . . at first. I did search, endlessly, but to no avail. Never to any avail."

"That's because Randegund lied to you," she said, her anger flaring over the witch's deceit. It was a good thing Alaric and Verica were keeping her well out of sight these days.

"True, it wasn't my fault, but at the time I blamed myself, and because of that, I did things, I allowed things to happen, I even pursued . . . " Magnus paused. "I used it as an excuse for all manner of excess, because I didn't want to know any more. I didn't want to think, or remember, or feel anything. It hurt too much."

Gigi shook her head, uneasy. *I finally have him talking*, she thought ironically, *and now I don't want to hear another word.* Apprehensive about what was coming next, she held her breath for a moment and then asked, "Such as?"

"Drinking, at first. Nearly constant drinking," he muttered. "I visited with my uncle and his family for a time, and he was very gracious and encouraging, but he was whole, and I was not. I didn't want to see his contentment again, so I left without saying a word.

"Once I was on the streets, my money held out for a time, but after weeks of debauchery, I did what I had to, to keep the drink coming. I sold my armor—I remember that—but then my memories fade."

Gigi had wondered about his missing armor, but there was an even greater question, and she feared the answer. "What happened to Agrippa?"

Magnus swung his legs out of the bed and sat up, his back to Gigi. He shook his head as if loathe to speak. "One morning, right toward the end, I woke up sick from too much drink and realized Agrippa was gone. I couldn't remember if I'd sold him, or if he'd been stolen. I still don't have any idea, but I had money in my pocket for the first time in weeks, so I must assume I sold my old friend. I keep imagining him strapped to a plow somewhere, whipped and abused, where once he'd been so proud and strong."

His voice caught and he cleared his throat, struggling to finish. "He saved my life more than once, and now, frequently, I wake up fearing I might have sold him to a . . . to a meat vendor."

"Oh, no," Gigi whispered in sorrow. She placed her arm around Magnus, hugging him, wanting to reassure. His skin felt cold, and he was trembling. "What can we do? Is there some way to find him?"

"No, he's gone."

It was what she expected to hear, but she went on anyway, "But what about your uncle? Couldn't he—"

"No, Gigi, no. Agrippa's gone."

"I'm sorry." Gigi shuddered, as much from his bitter tone as from the chilly air. Reaching for the blankets, she said, "Get back under the covers, Magnus. Come back to bed."

"No." He stopped her hand. "There's more, much more. For a time, I thought perhaps you'd gone back into the sparkling mist that brought you here, and I was desperate with the pain of losing you forever. So, I did things, things I'm not proud of."

Magnus's voice was so devoid of emotion, she realized she did not want him to go on, feared he was just getting to the crux of his heartache.

She looked into his eyes. "No more, please. It doesn't matter. It's in the past. Please, Magnus, I don't—"

"You must know everything, Gigi. I won't live under a falsehood. Afterward, the decision will be yours, whether to stay or go."

"What? No! Stop it, Magnus," Gigi said, sudden tears filling her eyes. "Don't you dare! I made my choice when we married. How can I—you thought I was dead, and I get it, but I don't want to hear it. Not another word."

"Gigi, I will not lie—"

"Stop!" She took his face in her hands. "I love you, and I'm no idiot, and I love you. That's all either of us needs to know. If you say another word, I swear I'll start screaming."

They stared at each other for several seconds, then, still holding him, Gigi took a long, calming breath. "It isn't lying and it's obviously no longer your dark secret, but I don't want specifics. I don't want details. If you unburden yourself, if you insist on this, then I am the one who will carry the burden forever. I have a vivid imagination, Magnus, and it will be inside my head for the rest of my life. Did she do it like this? Did you get turned on when she—"

"Gigi!"

"So, now you don't want to hear it," she persisted.

"No," he admitted.

"Good," she dropped her hands and forced a smile, "and please understand, given the circumstances there is nothing to forgive, but I do understand. I really do."

Magnus shook his head, then kissed her brow. "I need some fresh air." Getting up, he slung one of the furs over his shoulders for warmth and headed out of the tent.

Gigi watched him leave, and when the flap fell back into place, she started to shake, but not because of the cold. Silent tears fell, and she dropped onto the bed, his words and their significance running through her mind.

With sudden insight, she knew that for now he needed her to be strong for both of them. And he needed her forgiveness, wanted to hear the words, even if she couldn't listen to what he'd done, who he'd been with . . .

Another thought jolted her back to the moment. *What is he doing? Could he . . . ?*

Gigi got up and shoved her feet into her boots, grabbed her cloak and went out into the cold, wet night. Constantly wiping her face clear of pelting rain, she searched the common gathering places, then the alleyways between nearby tents. Running wildly, she splashed through puddles, looking everywhere, growing more frantic with each empty turn. Where was he?

Gigi halted at the edge of the camp, gasping for air. She saw his silhouette, black against the mist of rain, looking north over the Bay of Naples toward Capri, a place he loved. He must have heard her approach, for he glanced at her, but made no move in her direction.

"Magnus, why are you out here?" she asked. "Why are you punishing yourself like this? You can't just say stuff like that and then leave when I get upset. Give me a few moments, at least, before you run off to fall on your sword."

He looked at her curiously, then crossed his arms and turned back to the sea. "I did not kill myself when I feared you were lost to me forever, Gigi. I hadn't planned on killing myself now."

"Damn you, Magnus! Are you feeling sorry for yourself? Don't tell me—you're mad because I'm not letting you tell me every crude detail?" She got in his face and forced him to look at her. "Go confess your sins to Victoria if you want absolution on specifics, but don't expect it from me!"

"I'm not expecting absolution, Gigi. I have hated that you looked at me with such love, love I didn't deserve."

"But . . ." She took a deep breath, trying to focus her thoughts, because her next words were critical to their future. "You're not the one who gets to decide whether you deserve my love or not—that's my prerogative." Gigi drew the sodden cloak around her and then reached up to touch his face. "I'm sorry your grief drove you so far. But that doesn't change how I feel about you. Please, Magnus, I forgive you. I love you."

She fell quiet and he gazed at her, then nodded slightly, his expression relaxing into the barest of smiles.

"As you will," he said, "but the next time you run after me, all worked up and in a fright, first look to my weapons. Both my blades are still in the tent and plain to see. Besides, I made you a promise never to fall on my sword, and you may rest assured my oath binds me forever." He took her hand and kissed her ring. "I believe Victoria has guided me from the day you arrived in the baptistery, Gigi. It was my goddess who caused you to have the ring and brought you back in time. It was also Victoria who extricated me from a vile and unworthy emperor, whom I served because of a deathbed promise to his father, a good man who never guessed his young son would grow into a murderer without conscience."

"Magnus, I can't pretend to know why I'm here, but if it freed you from Honorius, then I'm glad."

He took her into his arms. "It was more than that, so much more." He kissed her, a long, lingering kiss that warmed her to her core. "I know now that my mission in life is to protect you. You are my wife, the only woman I have ever loved, and I will always stay by your side, no matter what happens. Shall we escape to the ends of the Earth, to that unknown continent of yours? Victoria will surely help. I shall make sacrifices to her at dawn. I will seek her guidance for a new start, asking the Fates to smile down upon us now and forever."

"Whatever happens, I love you, Magnus. I always will."

She nestled against him, willing herself to happiness, hoping it would turn out like they wanted, and that fate would be kind.

*

Honorius held his bird in his lap, cooing into her ear, "Ah, Rome, dearest pet, the city for which you were named has been destroyed. We must ask our astrologers what it portends, for you are precious to us." Hollow-eyed, he looked up at Sarus. "General, we would ask that you fetch our conjurers on your way out of our chambers."

Sarus stood there, feeling the crushing weight of contempt for Honorius, for much still needed to be discussed, including what should be done about King Alaric.

"Rome sacked!" Honorius started sniffling. "We would blame Olympius for this, but he is dead . . . dead. Oh, who is to blame? Who failed us?"

The emperor started blubbering and Sarus closed his eyes, taking a deep breath. He feared his life teetered on a knife's edge.

Olympius had been cruelly executed on a whim by Honorius, his ears cut off before he was clubbed to death in front of the entire court. Stilicho had been killed, too, as had so many others, too many.

Am I next? Sarus wondered, knowing full well once Honorius was done with his weeping, he'd lash out, placing blame on . . .

He let his breath out slowly, and then lowered himself to one knee, his hand over his chest. It was time to play his hand.

"O, Great Honorius, I have heard through my brother, Sergeric, that much more has happened in Rome. Prepare yourself, my lord, for the news is dire."

Honorius gaped, his fears unmasked. Sarus clung to his hope the little worm would finally give him leave to wreak vengeance against the man he blamed for the death of his wife and children, the one who had stolen the kingship from him, that bastard, Alaric. But would Honorius act against the news, or lash out against the messenger?

"What more?" the emperor's voice was a raspy whisper as he placed his bird on the floor and shooed her away. "Tell us, Sarus."

"Quintus Magnus returned to Rome just before the sack."

"Magnus?" Honorius's eyebrows raised in surprise.

Sarus nodded. "You know I had spies tailing him in Constantinople."

"Indeed, and we were quite vexed when your men could not find the right moment to slip him poison."

"*Venerabilis*, for that I apologize, but they lost track of Magnus after he sold his stallion to the horse master of the royal court. Magnus disappeared for months after that, only to show up in Rome. He and Gigiperrin were with your sister when she was taken hostage by Alaric's brother-in-law, Athaulf. It is said Magnus and the bitch flute player engineered your sister's capture, and Sergeric told me Athaulf and Placidia now share a tent—"

With a howl, Honorius grabbed Sarus by the throat. "What did you say? Is she fucking him?" he roared.

Sarus couldn't speak, tried to get hold of Honorius's hands, to push away and free himself. Suddenly, several of the imperial guards rushed into the room, and Sarus was knocked flat to the floor. Axes flashed, swam before his eyes, and he felt icy-cold metal pressing against his neck, the sting of the first cut. He was dead.

But Honorius blared, "Idiots, stand down! Let him go!"

Sarus was freed, then pulled to his feet by one of the guards.

Fingers trembling, he rubbed his neck, wiping away a trickle of blood.

Honorius was smiling as if nothing untoward had happened. "Come, General," he said, "we must put our heads together and hatch a plan. We were thwarted once before, but now it is time. We must kill our enemies—*all* of them—without delay. As for our sister, well, once she's brought home . . . in chains, perhaps, indeed, chains would be appropriate, we shall mete out her punishment. And then we'll hand her over to Constantius for marriage."

Honorius nodded, an exultant look in his eyes. "For too long our sister has acted willfully, not keeping to her place, and now she is no longer chaste. We intend to bring her low," he grinned, "by finding a way to cleanse her of the barbarian seed, perhaps supplanting it with the purity of Rome."

The emperor's gaze grew unfocused, and he touched himself.

The blame had been passed on to others. Sarus swallowed heavily in relief, but then shame swept over him as he recalled young Placidia's sweet gaze.

He closed his eyes, trying to force visions from his mind, depraved visions.

Heaven help the princess!

*

Athaulf stood outside his brother-in-law's tent, listening to him cough. As with so many in camp, it had gone on for weeks, although his fever had abated some time ago. "Alaric, it is Athaulf.

I would have a word."

"Come—"

Another fit of coughing interrupted the king's words, but Athaulf didn't wait. Asking leave to enter was only a formality. He found Magnus inside with Alaric, looking contented and thoughtful, but Verica and his mother were elsewhere. Perfect.

"Take your ease before me, brother." Clearing his throat, Alaric smiled and raised his golden goblet. "Get something to drink, and then pull up a chair."

Athaulf grabbed some beer and sat next to Magnus, then toasted the health of both men.

They all drank in silence, until Alaric wiped his mouth on his sleeve. "So, how goes the, er, peace negotiations between the noble Visigoth prince and Rome's fairest, er, maid?"

"Don't make light of this," Athaulf said seriously. "I want to marry her before our next move, and since officially she is our enemy, I feel I need your blessing upon the union, for the good of all. Otherwise, some might take it as an insult, and she might not be welcomed as she should."

"Do you refer to our mother?"

"Among others."

Alaric grimaced. "My blessing on your marriage will do nothing to placate Randegund. In truth, I fear nothing will placate her now that her mind is tortured by . . . demons," he sighed, "but I—"

"King Alaric," a sentry interrupted from outside, "there is a Roman soldier here with a package, one which must be delivered in person to your brother. May he enter?"

"If he is unarmed, of course," Alaric called out, "let him in."

Wary, Athaulf stood, wondering who among the Romans might send him something, and Magnus and Alaric rose to stand beside him.

A common soldier entered, looking haughty and unabashed at being at the very center of his enemy's encampment. He glanced at the three men, his air of disdain obvious when he recognized

Magnus. Then, assessing height differences between Athaulf and Alaric, he turned to Athaulf and held out a small crate, bound with leather straps and sealed with wax.

"You are the shorter of the two, so I take it you are Athaulf?" he asked.

Athaulf acknowledged the fact with a slight nod. "Who sends this, and what is it?"

"As to what it is, I wasn't informed," the man said coolly. "The sender is none other than Flavius Honorius Augustus, Emperor of Rome."

Troubled, Athaulf glanced at Alaric and Magnus, then took the proffered box. He pulled out his knife and cut the straps, then pried off the lid. The interior held a glass jar, tightly packed in straw.

Magnus stepped forward. "Leave it, Athaulf. This is some twisted jest."

"There is a note," Athaulf said.

Magnus reached in, snatched the small piece of parchment, and read it in silence.

"What does it say?" Alaric asked, stepping toward him.

Magnus's lips tightened. "When you fuck Rome, Rome will fuck you."

Furious, Athaulf spun around to demand an explanation, but the Roman soldier had already slipped out of the tent.

Athaulf pulled forth the jar and peered at its contents, then recoiled and cursed in anger. A shriveled, blackened head floated inside, a young boy's head, and a tag read, "*Eucherius, son of Stilicho.*"

Magnus grabbed the jar and quickly put it back in the box.

Alaric's gaze was filled with disgust. "Truly, Honorius is deranged."

"Eucherius must be buried," Magnus said emotionally. "It is little enough we can do to honor the poor child."

"I shall marry her, Alaric," Athaulf insisted. "Placidia must never fall into the hands of that monster. Never! I will not allow that beast to have sway over her again. I will protect her with my love, and with my sword."

"Say nothing to her about this," Magnus warned. "Nothing—ever. She must never know."

"Tomorrow, brother," Alaric said quietly. "I will tell Verica to make everything ready. You may wed the girl tomorrow."

*

Placidia felt breathless with joy. Athaulf had come in late in the night and held her so closely, so tenderly, as though she might slip away without warning. Then, as dawn lightened the sky, he'd asked her to marry him—without delay—and now, here she was, looking at her bridegroom through an orange veil.

The Arian bishop had just made the pronouncement, declared them wed. Never again would she be beholden to Honori—*no!* she scolded herself. She mustn't even think the name, not on this perfect, perfect day. It was a time for new beginnings.

Athaulf lifted the veil and smiled at her.

My husband! To think we found love amid the ashes, after the fall of Rome. Together, we will make a future, together always . . .

She smiled back. "I love you, Athaulf. I am so proud to be your wife."

He leaned down and kissed her, gently at first, then scooped her into his arms, lifting her off her feet, and kissed her more deeply.

When he set her back down, everyone was cheering and applauding, Gigi and Magnus most of all. Placidia reached out and took Gigi's hand.

"I'm not jealous of your love any longer, Gigi," she cried out, smiling through tears of joy, trying to make herself heard over the noise. "My heart is so full!"

Gigi laughed and started to say something, but Athaulf took hold of Placidia's hand, pulling her toward their tent and the blessing the bishop would pronounce over it.

She hurried beside her new husband, his big, reassuring hand grasping hers, as though he would never let go. She had always known she would marry a prince of a foreign nation, a non-Roman, and that much was true.

She had never once thought love would have anything to do with it.

Chapter 13

Shielding her eyes against the driving rain, Gigi looked out over the rough sea, the waves wind-whipped and streaming foam. Hundreds of watercraft of every shape and description were still in the bay and getting thrashed by the storm. Some, loaded with soldiers and horses, were already struggling to make it across the Strait of Messina.

Alaric had made agreements with the people of Rhegium and the surrounding hamlets for anyone owning a boat to help transport the Visigoths to Sicily, where he planned to spend the winter. Southern Italy was played out, and his people faced starvation. In the spring, the king would lead them from Sicily to northern Africa, Italy's breadbasket. They would take the grain supply by force, thus putting a stranglehold on the Western Roman Empire, driving her once and for all to her knees. There was also talk they might permanently settle in Africa, which was why Rhegium gladly agreed to help, hoping to see the swift departure of the voracious barbarians, who had already picked their fields, vineyards, and flocks down to stubble and bone.

Farther downhill, pacing, Magnus looked as uneasy as Gigi felt. That morning, he'd asked her what she knew of this plan, if to her knowledge it had worked, but she didn't have any idea. History was not her thing, after all. She'd only vaguely remembered hearing about the sack of Rome, her grandfather saying it was the beginning of the end of antiquity. But as for details about crossing the strait, she recalled nothing.

Gigi caught some movement and looked to see Magnus climbing the short rise to join her. His brow was creased with worry when he got to her side.

"Alaric has left a small contingent of soldiers for the last boat," he said, "to protect the women and children on this end. For now, the bulk of the force will cross, then provisions and most of the animals, then women, children, and the infirm. It will take most of the day."

She looked up at him. "With this weather, and those boats having to do roundtrips, I'd guess it will take a couple of days."

"I fear you are right. The king keeps telling himself the wind will hurry the process." Magnus shook his head. "He's not in his right mind. I can't understand this decision, this urgency to get across, especially in these conditions."

"He's been sick for ages."

"Everybody's been sick for ages, and he's been sick often enough before this. That's never stopped him from thinking clearly."

Gigi shrugged. "I don't like this. I wouldn't try this crossing on a day like today in a Beneteau, let alone the rickety stuff he's got out there."

"A Beneteau?" He looked at her with curiosity. "A sailing ship from the future?"

"Indeed, and a very good one," Gigi smiled grimly, "but I still wouldn't go out today."

Magnus turned back to the sea. "I have asked to go with the last of the soldiers, to be closer to you and Placidia."

Gigi glanced at him, but he was watching the pier where the boats were being loaded. It had been nearly a week since he'd unburdened himself to her, and no matter how much she tried to make him realize it was all in the past, he was still angry with himself.

But today was different. This was scary, and she couldn't allow him to go on like this. Reaching out, she put her hand in his and his fingers closed around hers at once.

"I love you, Magnus," she said. "Don't ever doubt that, not for a moment."

He nodded and opened his mouth to say something, but thought better of it and simply squeezed her hand. They stood like that for some time, watching as more and more heavily loaded craft dotted the strait. Sicily's highest peaks had been shrouded in rain clouds all day, but now Gigi noticed the mist had descended lower still. The whole island was difficult to make out, the clouds darker and more threatening.

Gigi clutched his arm and cried out. A sudden squall was kicking up heavy seas, and boats slammed against one another. Several capsized, while others were listing.

Magnus saw it, too, and started running down the hillside.

Gigi followed as lightning flashed across the sky, and the heavy rain picked up its intensity, the gusts sending it sideways. Wiping the rain from her eyes, Gigi tried to see what was going on. Overhead, thunder boomed, and she stumbled and fell.

Three more boats pitched over in the swells, men and horses flailing, their screams rising above the howling wind. She got up and ran on. Magnus was headed for the end of the pier and she followed.

Frozen in shock, Verica stood with dozens of others. "Their boat—Alaric's boat," she sobbed.

"Stay here," Gigi ordered, "and do not move. Stay where I can find you."

Stricken, the queen nodded, and Gigi pushed her way through the horrified crowd, grabbing people she knew, giving orders. "Get everyone back. Make room to bring the survivors on shore." "Get help—get supplies—blankets—*now*." "Don't panic—whatever you do—they need you to be strong."

Gigi spotted Placidia scrambling down the jagged boulders underpinning the pier. Another bolt of lightning made Gigi's hair stand on end, and the thunderclap hit almost simultaneously, nearly knocking the breath out of her.

"Placidia, no!" she yelled just as the princess fell between the boulders. The sea surged over her, her arms flailing to find something to grab and hold.

Gigi hurried over the slick rocks, desperate to reach her. As the wave receded, she glimpsed Placidia's terror-filled gaze. "Placidia!"

Gigi lunged for the princess as another wave hit, slamming her against a boulder—but she had a hand! She had Placidia! Pulling with all her strength, Gigi hauled her onto solid footing, but Placida immediately tried to head back to the rocks.

Gigi held her fast, shouting, "What are you doing?"

"Athaulf's boat—I must help—my husband is in the water. Let me go—"

"No, Placidia! The surf will kill you. You'll be no help, and when he swims ashore he'll find you dead."

The words must have sunk in, because Placidia stared at Gigi, eyes wide with fright. "But . . . I can't do nothing," she wept. "I can't just stand by and watch."

Struggling for a response, Gigi looked around and then spotted some women praying on a nearby hill.

"Placidia, get Verica and go up on that hill and pray. You can't jump in the water and kill yourself. I won't allow it!"

There was a flicker in Placidia's eyes and then she was gone, thankfully toward the hill this time.

Shouts. Screams. Gigi ran toward the end of the pier. Waves crested, crashing across the top, driving people to their knees, and sweeping some into the sea. Hulls of overturned boats rose up, only to disappear again.

Pushing her way forward, she finally reached Magnus, who was grasping at swimmers and bodies alike, trying to get them out. Helping where she could, she glanced back, and saw most of the people had retreated. Some were on the hill praying with Placidia and Verica, and she spotted Randegund with them, arms raised, her white hair whipping in the wind.

Along the beach, people helped survivors get ashore. Gigi saw a horse rise out of the waves, stumble across the sand, and dash up the hillside.

"Magnus," she yelled, "we should go to the beaches!"

But he was staring out to sea, a look of shock on his face. Gigi followed his gaze and cried out. Athaulf, Alaric, and another man clung to an overturned boat, the sea roiling around them. Athaulf's head was up, but not Alaric's, and Athaulf had a death grip on the king's arm.

Magnus started for the water, but Gigi grasped his arm. "You can't help them. You'll die if you go in there!" He struggled against her, but she refused to let go. "You'll take me with you if you go in—you choose!"

He glared at her, then looked to where she pointed along the shore.

"Over there," she shouted. "The surf is pushing them over there."

He nodded, and they ran down the pier together, reaching the beach just as lightning crashed somewhere close. The atmosphere reeked of sulfur as thunder shook the earth. The surf pounded the shore, great sprays of saltwater filling the air, and Gigi could see huge boulders just off the beach. Even if Alaric and Athaulf survived the rough seas, they would have a terrible time avoiding the rocks. The beach was already littered with pieces of boats and rigging, and there were bodies everywhere.

While Magnus kept watch for Athaulf, Gigi hurried among the debris, turning bodies over and checking for signs of life. When one man threw up a stomach full of seawater, she waved for help, and soon he was taken away to be treated.

Gigi continued to search, finding several corpses beneath planks or tangled up in ropes, and then she came upon someone with an ugly, bleeding gash on his head, making her think he wouldn't last much longer.

She heard yelling, and turned to see a bare-chested Magnus start to wade into the angry surf. "No!" she screamed. "Magnus, don't!"

Gigi ran after him, following him in up to her knees, trying to pull him back, but he wouldn't be stopped this time, and Gigi saw why—Athaulf was swimming in, his head nearly submerged, and he was dragging Alaric's limp body behind him. There was no sign of the third person she'd seen on the boat.

The riptide was fierce, nearly yanking her feet out from beneath her, and Gigi was helpless to do anything but save herself. She struggled back until the water was at her ankles, but when a big wave surged in, she turned and ran. Stumbling against something, she looked down and saw Magnus's abandoned tunic and boots. Terrified by his daring, she took his clothes and hugged them to her chest, her cries carried away by the ocean's roar.

Magnus drove forward through the surf, inch by inch, until he reached Athaulf. Grabbing hold of Alaric, he hauled both men back toward land.

Gigi dropped Magnus's things and raced forward. By the time he reached her, Placidia and Verica were also in the water beside them, grasping for their men, dragging them onto the sand. Once ashore, Athaulf collapsed from exhaustion into Placidia's arms, while Magnus and Verica pushed Alaric onto his stomach and pounded his back.

Anxious over their futile efforts, Gigi suddenly felt a presence, something bitter, vile. Looking up, she spotted Randegund again. The old woman wasn't praying any more, just glaring down from the cliffs, rigid except for her wind-lashed hair, which lifted and flailed, snakelike.

Oh, Medusa has nothing on that bitch! Empowered, she turned back to Alaric. *Okay, Gigi,* she told herself, *you took first aid as a Girl Scout—remember what they taught you.*

"Turn him over," she commanded Magnus and Verica. "I know what to do."

Gigi balled up her fists and plunged her body weight against the king's stomach, then heaved him over on his side. Water gushed out, but he wasn't choking on it, so she did it again, this time getting some help from Magnus. Then she quickly tilted Alaric's head back and looked at her husband. "You pinch his nose with one hand, clamp down his tongue with the other, and give him three deep breaths when I tell you."

Arms rigid, thumbs linked, Gigi rose up on her knees beside Alaric and started pumping on his breastbone, *one, two, three, four* . . . "Now, Magnus, breathe!" she yelled. *One, two, three, four* . . . "Breathe!" *One, two, three, four* . . . "Breathe!"

Again, Gigi balled her fists, this time coming down on Alaric's chest with all her force, furious with him for not responding. *"Goddamnit, breathe!"* she screamed in English, then resumed the CPR, her arms and shoulders leaden, burning with the effort. *One, two, three—*

"Gigi!" Verica grabbed her arm just as Alaric seized, lurched sideways, and spewed more water out of his body.

Stunned, Gigi stared at Alaric as he labored to suck in air, his eyes wide with the effort to survive. It had worked!

Numb, cold, and shaking, Gigi rose and stood in the midst of the carnage, only then realizing the magnitude of what she'd done in saving a king's life.

She glanced at Magnus. Having risen with her, he looked amazed and proud.

Gigi threw her arms around his neck. "M—Magnus," she said through chattering teeth.

He held her tightly. "Bravely borne, my love," he whispered into her hair. "You shouldered the burden of a grievous day and kept it from being far worse. Sweet Victory has granted us all another dawn."

"Victory," she affirmed and nestled against him, "but not just mine. We did it together, Magnus."

Chapter 14

The wind blew fierce, smelling of snow, as Gigi said goodbye to Placidia and started for home. After a day spent watching Athaulf's children, she looked forward to getting back to the quiet of her own tent. The ever-patient princess was proving to be a great stepmother, and Athaulf's little girls thoroughly enjoyed playing dress-up with her fabulous jewels and silks. As for the boys, Athaulf insisted they get civilized by taking advantage of Gigi's musical talent. She had fought with them over this for days, finally reaching an uneasy truce—equal hours of music for swordplay—their precondition being that if they had to do her bidding, she had to do theirs. At first, the little demons ran rings around her, constantly whacking her backside with their wooden swords, but now she was finally getting the hang of it, and their butts were just as sore.

Unfortunately, Athaulf's sons showed little promise of becoming the next great boy band, but she was determined to get them ready to perform at the coming banquet to celebrate Alaric's survival. Something from the Jonas Brothers? Or maybe Justin Bieber?

Whatever, they're kids. They'll be a hit no matter what, she thought with a smile. They would certainly be better than Alaric's minstrels, who sang nothing but the same bloodthirsty war ballads over and over again. *Truly barbarous*, she thought with a smile.

Despite their Visigoth heritage, Athaulf had allowed his sons to be "Romanized" to a degree, encouraging their education in the Latin language, Roman history and Greek philosophy, but he had not relented in one thoroughly Roman requirement of childhood: the bulla. It was a locket worn by Roman boys to ward off evil spirits. Gigi had overhead Placidia requesting that he consider bestowing the amulets on his children, to no avail. She wondered if Athaulf would eventually relent. *Wait and see*, she told herself, knowing how much it would mean to Placidia.

She blew into her hands, picking up her pace. Pushing on her tent flap, she stepped inside, trying to ignore the first twinges of a sinus headache. Rubbing her brow, she wished she could pop into a drugstore and get what she needed. She hadn't told Verica, not wanting anything to do with the foul tasting, slimy-green potion she usually doled out as a cure-all.

Crawling into bed, she burrowed under the furs and closed her eyes. It was ironic, but people were now coming to her for medical advice, since the strange new role of miracle worker had been foisted on her after Alaric's CPR. These days, the awestruck Visigoths made way as she walked by, as if she were a life-renewing goddess. They'd even started asking her for favors, such as the blessing of their children. It was weird and unnerving, but nice just the same. Many were reminded of her arrival among them, posing as High Priestess of the Old Ones, and believed it was her true identity.

Yet still, only Magnus knew her truth. She couldn't risk telling anyone else, although Placidia had asked her point-blank where she'd learned how to bring a drowned man back to life. Gigi smiled, recalling how she'd scrambled for an answer, but then realized the simple truth was good enough, telling her it was a common practice among sailors. She even offered to teach her the method, but Placidia demurred, saying she hoped they would never again travel anywhere by ship. The recent sea disaster had killed many and devastated everyone in the camp, but at least there was one ray of hope: Alaric was getting better day by day, lovingly tended by Verica and Randegund.

Those haunting blue eyes, frightening in their intensity, were always hate-filled and all-consuming. Chained to her memories, Gigi shivered. More than once since Alaric's near-drowning, she'd caught Randegund staring at her, and she felt it acutely, as if the old bitch wanted to murder her with her gaze.

But why? Why? I saved Alaric's life, she argued inwardly. *You'd think she'd be grateful.*

She turned her face into the furs, snuggling deeper, her headache fading, her fears threatening her still. She needed to forget Randegund. Gigi and Magnus had each other, and the bitch couldn't hurt them anymore. Her children were seeing to that.

Her thoughts roamed on to more pleasant things. She had her music, plus theirs, so many wonderful ancient melodies. And Placidia was going to take them to Hadrian's Villa for the winter, where plenty of food was stored, and there would be shelter enough for everyone. After that, when Alaric led his people to their new homeland in Africa, then maybe she and Magnus could take a little side trip to Capri, even go to southern France. Or . . . ?

"Gigi, where are you?"

She roused herself, just as Magnus entered their tent. She smiled at him, stretching luxuriously, but then caught herself, recognizing something in his expression, something she hadn't wanted to see ever again.

"The king," his voice was halting, anguished. "Alaric has taken a bad turn."

She couldn't believe it. When she'd seen him a few hours earlier, he'd looked so much better. He still had a slight cough, but he was sitting up in bed, and he'd gotten his color back. Verica had just given him a big spoonful of honey, and for the first time in days, he was asking for something hearty to eat, to replace the gruel and soup she'd been feeding him.

"Verica said you must come quickly," Magnus went on. "Alaric's lungs have filled with fluid."

Pneumonia? Shocked, Gigi threw off the covers, wondering what she could do, how in the world she could help.

Magnus took her hand, and together they left on the run.

*

Randegund exited the stuffy sick tent and took a deep breath, seeking revival in the cool night air. Overhead, the sky was coal-dark, the stars distant white fire. She felt shriveled, ancient, and weary, a husk of her former self and overwhelmed by uselessness, for Alaric was dying, and she knew not what to do.

Once she was well away from the camp, she halted and prayed to the ancient Goddess of Revenge, whispering to the night sky, "Mighty Nemesis, winged avenger, dark-faced Goddess of Justice! Fly through the night to the tent of my beloved chosen son, Alaric. Witness the evil done him, hear his agony. I ask—I *plead*—for retribution against Quintus Pontius Flavus Magnus and his wife, Gigi, for they alone are responsible for Alaric's pain, having denied him the nobility of a heroic end."

Her voice was drowned out by the rising wind, and she swore she heard the deep *whoosh* of wings. "Implacable Daughter of Vengeance," she said, raising her voice, howling to the roiling sky, "fly, fly to Alaric's side! If it be your will, Great Nemesis, save him. But if he is meant to die, then hunt down his killers. Avenge him! Fly, fly!"

Bending into the wind, Randegund fought the weakness of her aged limbs and slowly retraced her steps to Alaric's tent. Near the entrance, Verica stood with Gigi, Magnus, and the Roman whore, Placidia. The women were huddled together, holding each other, weeping.

Why had Verica called them here? Disgusted, Randegund drew back, hastening to the shadows. How could her daughter be so trusting, so utterly stupid? She shook her head, wondering why Verica loved these Romans—she leaned over and spat—wishing she could hear what they were saying to each other.

I may yet cut out Gigi's impudent tongue, if she dares make another excuse as to why Alaric was left to flounder so long in the sea, when she and Magnus knew—they knew—he was drowning. And as for the Roman princess-bitch who has bewitched my Athaulf . . .

There was a sudden commotion from the tent, a deep moan of anguish. The need to be at Alaric's side superseded her hatred and her aching bones, and Randegund hobbled forward as fast as she could go.

Sweeping past the small group, she pointed to her enemies, and cried out, "You are not wanted here! Go away!"

Entering the tent, Verica fast on her heels, she found Athaulf at the sickbed, his arm around young Theodoric's trembling shoulders. The other children were huddled in a corner, silent and pale.

Randegund pushed her way to Alaric's bedside and fell to her knees, taking his hand in her own. Alaric's face was paler than before, the skin a sickly yellow, his hands and arms mottled, purple. Death was near.

With a great effort, he opened his eyes and whispered, "Athaulf."

Then his chest was seized with liquid rattles and he struggled, wheezing, "Mother, I see her!"

A convulsion passed through him, then a shudder, and Alaric died, his final breath gurgling away to nothing.

Randegund raised her hands in tribute to the departing soul and began to chant. She could feel eyes on the back of her skull, but she kept her gaze locked on Alaric's beloved face—his death-face. She knew what they were thinking, knew they'd forsworn such rituals as nonsense years before, but they were wrong. She reveled in the knowledge his death vision hadn't been of his birth mother or of any other woman. He had seen Nemesis just before he crossed to the darkness of the Otherworld, of that she was certain!

The Otherworld! My Alaric! The sudden realization he was truly and forever gone struck hard and her arms dropped to her side. Randegund cried for him and for herself, feeling as she always had, that he was her blood son, her own flesh, sinew, and bone. In truth, he had been more important to her than anyone in the world.

And now he was gone, and she knew her life was over, the agony tearing through her, unbearable.

Weeping, she kissed Alaric's lifeless hand, carefully positioning it with the other, folding them both on his chest, over his heart. With a final kiss to his brow, she closed his eyes. Rising, she looked around to see her wailing daughter, a widow too soon, the others sobbing in grief, and her heart filled with an icy, silent intent. She shivered, then wiped her eyes and shook herself free from fear, feeling curiously renewed, as if a divine power had entered her body.

There was but one thing left to do in her life, a final act of vengeance, and she knew Nemesis was with her, deep inside her breast, waiting for the right moment to strike.

*

It was a fine day in winter's depth, the sky clear, cold, and blue, achingly blue.

Gigi stood with Placidia at a bend in the river Busentinus, overlooking the burial site of King Alaric. She was bundled in a heavy wool cloak; the princess decked out in sumptuous furs and her imperial regalia, including a delicate golden crown glittering with sapphires, called the Crown of Livia, she'd said. They held hands and listened to the eerie caterwauls of the women closest to Alaric, their grief echoing off the surrounding rocks, cries of doom.

Hundreds of slaves had toiled for the past week to build a huge log dam to divert the river, so Alaric's corpse and a vast amount of treasure could be interred beneath the riverbed. The tomb had been dug into solid bedrock and would be covered with slabs of purest white marble. Afterward, the waters would be channeled back to their original course, and the grave would be inviolate, hidden from Honorius's desire to despoil, from Catholic avengers, and from pagans still livid over the Visigoth desecrations during the sack of Rome.

Both Gigi and Placidia wept as they watched a slow procession of Alaric's male relatives and friends, Athaulf and Magnus chief among them, convey the body to the tomb. The dead king had been regally dressed in purple brocade, the fabulous gem-encrusted goblet folded within the stillness of his hands.

Holding a large gold cross before him, the Arian bishop waited by the funeral bier, as the pallbearers carefully lowered the body, then stood in silence.

The bishop raised his voice, "King of the Visigoths! Long may you dwell in the sight of the Heavenly Throne of our Lord God, the Unbegotten One, and his son, Jesus, the Begotten!"

Mournful cries swelled to a crescendo as Randegund led the women in the cutting of their braids and maidenly tresses. Keening and weeping, they flung their shorn hair toward the riverbed, to rest as tribute at the base of Alaric's tomb.

Gigi wiped away tears as Verica cut Berga's hair, and then motioned for the child to take it to her father's side. The girl looked frightened as she approached the bier, her hands shaking as she halted and glanced at her mother for reassurance. When Verica nodded, Berga turned and flung her hair high, the pale blond wisps catching on Alaric's cup-laden hands, curling around them. Verica dropped to her knees, holding Berga in a silent, tearful vigil.

"Cruel, cruel fate," Placidia sadly whispered, and Gigi wondered if she were speaking of Athaulf as well. The princess's handsome husband was now de facto ruler of the Visigoths, and from the abounding gossip in the camp, Gigi guessed almost everyone was going to vote for him, giving him the kingship. His fate was sealed, his coming responsibilities huge and grave. Gigi knew Placidia realized this as well.

"I understand," Gigi whispered back as she clung to the princess's trembling hand, wishing she had listened more carefully to her grandfather's tales of Rome. If somehow, some way she had been able to replay his stories in her mind, then she might have warned Alaric of the sea disaster, perhaps averting his premature death. And she would know her friends' fates, Placidia and Athaulf's future.

More tears rolled down her cheeks. *Why didn't I listen? It would have made Grand-père so happy, and now, what's going to happen now?*

*

she tried to wriggle free, but it was futile. "Magnus, let go of me!"

"I love you, but . . . " His voice was low, implacable. "As your husband, I demand your obedience in this. Do not tell anyone, certainly not her. *Ever.*"

He released her. Blinded by tears, she fell sobbing onto the bed. Later, she could not recall how long it was before he left, or if he'd said anything more.

*

Night, that great dark beast, crept over the land. In the shadows, Randegund sat in her tent, stirring sleeping powder into a cup of blood-red wine.

Black thoughts hit her like wind gusts, tearing at her soul. *O, Despoiler Romans, Most Hated Ones! You who stood amongst us when my beloved foster-son, Alaric, was laid to rest. Magnus! Gigi! Placidia!*

She saw it all again, unbidden memories, the travesty of this day. *How dare you act the Visigoth and carry his body, Magnus! Defiler! And you, Gigi, how dare you give Placidia your dagger, so the princess-whore could pollute my precious son's grave with her filthy Roman hair! How dare you take Verica in your arms, Placidia, and declare yourself one of us! Athaulf's true wife rests in her grave in Noricum. In my eyes, you are nothing compared to her. Nothing!*

She balled her fists, squeezing them until the nails bit into her skin and she bled. But how could she get to them? Those three were too well protected by their guile, and by her foolish, misguided children, Athaulf and Verica.

By the Furies, she had to find a way to rid her people of the Roman infiltrators. Would that they were included with the slaves at the river and butchered this day. How she would have loved to do it herself!

Hands shaking, Randegund took up the wine potion, cursing as she spilt some on herself. Her daughter would have need of it in the coming nights and none must be wasted, for Verica was bereft, sick with grief.

As are we all, Randegund bitterly thought. Unbidden tears sprang to her eyes, and she let them course down her face, watching as they fell into the potion and mingled with its secrets.

What would you do? she asked, touching her breast.

But Nemesis did not stir.

Randegund almost flung the cup in outrage, but fought with herself for patience. The goddess would answer in her own time.

She took the potion and carefully placed it on a table. *Verica, only daughter of my womb, who does not easily thank me or care for my regard any more. These days, you have other concerns, other loves.*

And Alaric's love was no more. He was gone. Dead.

All because of them!

Sitting in the gloom, Randegund placed her hands over her ears, rocking to and fro, repeating the names, hating the names. *Roman filth! Magnus! Gigi! Placidia!* Her anger redoubled, and she leapt up, her fury imparting a strength she hadn't felt in years. A blood sacrifice would serve as a balm both to her and Nemesis.

With a cry, she reached for her knife and stormed outside.

*

Sergeric wiped his sweaty hands on his tunic, hating the creepy darkness of these southern woods, hating even more the Romans with whom he had been ordered to meet. *Imperial spies—shit-eating Roman dogs!*

He slipped unnoticed past the outermost ring of sentries, heading for an ancient oak, the meeting place according to his elder brother's secret missive. *Sarus must know what he is doing,* he told himself, *even if I do not understand why he would ask me to risk so much.*

Eyes straining against the dark, Sergeric crept forward until he spotted the silhouette of a great tree, bare branches twisting toward the star-filled sky. He halted and looked around. Unnerved, he felt as if the eyes of his people were watching his deeds, waiting to strike. Treason would bring a horrible end, mutilation first, the removal of the eyes, nose, ears, and tongue, then death by strangulation.

He took a deep breath and let it out slowly, berating himself for allowing fear to rule his heart, and for questioning his elder brother's intentions. His loyalty to Sarus superseded all else, yet he was plagued with doubt just the same. What was his brother thinking? After all, time was on their side. Alaric was dead, and Sergeric was about to make a move for the kingship. Many said they would vote for him, for there was a groundswell of ill feeling toward Athaulf, because of Placidia.

Suddenly, there was a rustling of leaves, the faintest sound.

Wary, Sergeric touched his sword hilt as two shadowy figures appeared from the deeper gloom of the forest.

"Sarus is our general," one of the men whispered to him.

"Sarus is my brother," Sergeric answered back.

*

Randegund stood in the dark, gripping her knife. She could smell the Romans in her midst, the sweet stink of their fish sauce, the repulsive *garum*, filling the air.

She glanced at the goat she had ritually slaughtered. It lay in the shadows near the mighty, sacred oak, her pleas and prayers at its killing a silent testament to the power of the gods. Smiling, she thanked them again, for she knew her sacrifice had brought forth these Romans, who now huddled together, the scum.

They were speaking in whispers, but she cared not what they said. She would get her revenge on them this night, a poor substitute for her real enemies, but a substitute nonetheless.

Raising her knife, she inched forward, about to strike, when one voice rose above the whisperings, "The general's instructions were exactly as stated, Sergeric. By whatever means possible, capture Quintus Pontius Flavus Magnus and his wife. Bring them to us for transport to Ravenna."

"But how?" Sergeric asked in confusion.

"By whatever means possible," came the angry reply. "The emperor has special need of them, as entertainment for games he will hold in celebration of Alaric's death."

Randegund froze. *Bastard of Rome!* she wanted to scream. *Would that I could slit your throat and bathe in your blood, Honorius. I would gladly feed your eyes, tongue, and cock to the crows!*

She used all her strength to control her rage, for the gods were kind, and they would strike the foul emperor in time. As for Magnus and his bitch-wife, they were to be taken to him. Oh, would that she could see with her own eyes what he had in store for them. This was the answer to her prayers.

But the stupid oaf, Sergeric, must be assisted in this, otherwise he would surely spoil the plan. She stared at the three black figures, hating them all, but most especially the miserable traitor. Yet now she would use him for her own ends, her mind awhirl.

By whatever means possible . . .

She lowered her knife, the itch to kill gone, replaced by a renewed desire for the settling of scores. She would go to Sergeric's tent this night and provide him the sleeping draught to use on Magnus and his wife.

Touching her chest, she pleaded for the help of the Great Winged Avenger. And this time Nemesis answered back, for Randegund felt a strange fluttering, followed by a twinge in her breast, near the place where her heart drummed. She understood what it meant: her call to battle.

Chapter 16

Agitated, Gigi had left her tent, only to spend sleepless hours in Verica's. She rolled over and opened her eyes. The dim light of a lone oil lamp pierced the gloom, and shadows flickered, wavering like ghosts. She shivered, watching Randegund. The old woman had crept in after everyone was asleep and hadn't noticed Gigi. Now, she slept beside Verica, who was drugged with one of Randegund's potions. Several other women were scattered about on cots, and looked to be sleeping peacefully enough. Like Verica and Randegund, their hair was shorn, spiky and uneven. It would take a while for Gigi to get used to seeing them this way.

Her gaze was drawn back to Randegund, and she recalled the first time she'd seen her over two years before. She was strangely beautiful then, her hair long and pure white, her blue eyes mesmerizing and fierce. But now, without the great mane, the acid glare, she looked pitiable, like the shriveled, decrepit old woman she was. Regardless, Gigi knew better than to turn her back on such hatred.

Another shiver and she pulled the covers close. She wished she could sleep . . . she was so tired . . . but she didn't dare take her eyes off Randegund, who'd probably stab her, if given half a chance. She wished Placidia was with her, but Verica hadn't wanted the reminder, since Placidia was now effectively the queen of the Visigoths.

Poor Placidia. If she ever found out what Athaulf had done . . .

In turmoil, Gigi sat up. *How long does it take to murder that many people? Are they done yet, or are they still at it? What will Magnus be like when he gets back, how messed up?*

Rubbing her eyes, Gigi regretted having argued with him. There was nothing he could have done. All she wanted right now was his soothing presence, his strong arms wrapped tightly around her.

Pulling on her boots, she crept out of Verica's tent and slipped into her own. In the faint light, she was surprised to find their bed empty, then recalled telling him not to return that night. Glancing around, she could see the tent wasn't as she'd left it. Obviously, Magnus had come back, his blades and cloak stowed in the corner, a mug of wine on the table, another lying on the floor near the bed, the wine spilled. Gigi grew uneasy, wondering at the overturned mug. Where had he gone? Why hadn't he looked for her among the women? Was he ill?

She checked the nearest latrine, but it was empty, then one farther off, also empty. Fighting panic, she hurried toward Athaulf's tent, reassuring herself she'd find him there. She passed the occasional night sentry, but no one else. It had to be well past midnight, she decided, because so few were around. Her concern grew when she saw there was no light showing beneath the skins. "Athaulf?" She knocked on a pole, then called out softly, "Placidia, is Magnus in there? Athaulf, where is Magnus?"

"Gigi?" Placidia's muffled, sleepy voice sounded confused.

She heard movement in the tent, and moments later Athaulf was before her, looking rumpled. "What's this about?" he asked with a yawn.

"I can't find Magnus!" Gigi heard the rising panic in her voice, but didn't care if she woke up the entire camp now. "He came back to the tent, but he's not there anymore."

Athaulf frowned. "Not there? He told me he was heading home, that he needed to make things right with you."

"I've been with Verica the whole time, but he never went there—I would've seen him. Something's not right. Please, help me find him."

Athaulf disappeared inside, then returned almost immediately, fully dressed. "Is my mother with Verica?"

Gigi nodded. "She's in Verica's tent."

Athaulf set off without waiting to hear more, Gigi close on his heels as he burst inside the tent.

"Mother!" he bellowed, sending several women scrambling, but Verica and Randegund slept on. Athaulf was across the tent in a few strides and threw back his mother's blankets. "Mother, wake up!"

Her eyes flew open and she cowered for a moment, but then her gaze grew hard and she sat up, glaring and undaunted. "Why would you ruin a mournful old woman's sleep?" she griped.

"Because the old woman is endlessly duplicitous," Athaulf replied sharply. "Where is Magnus? What have you done?"

Gigi expected Randegund to deny any knowledge of his whereabouts, but a smile pushed back her wrinkles. In fear, Gigi sucked in her breath at the vision of pure hatred.

"Magnus is our bane, Athaulf, though you refuse to acknowledge this fact," Randegund said. "Ill-fate and ruin have dogged our every step since he first came into our lives so many years ago. It was time to deal with him."

Crying out, Gigi lunged at her, but Athaulf blocked her path.

Randegund's eyes flickered toward the movement, her brows lowered over a venomous glare. "Oh, he still lives. I tried to rid us of his whore as well, but no matter, her fate will be sealed soon enough."

"No!" Gigi yelled, struggling to get at her, but Athaulf held her fast.

"Where is Magnus, Mother? Where?"

Randegund grinned. "I slipped some of Verica's sleeping draught into wine I left for them. At this moment he is amongst his own—though he won't be aware of it yet—being taken back to his beloved emperor," Randegund spat on the floor of the tent, "to Honorius in Ravenna."

"*You bitch!*" Gigi screamed in English, then lunged at Randegund, but Athaulf wouldn't let go.

Randegund shrieked with laughter.

"Get you gone, old woman," he bellowed to his mother. "*You* are the poison in our midst. Magnus never was."

Athaulf forced Gigi out of Verica's tent.

"Let me go, Athaulf! I need a horse—I have to help Magnus!"

He shook his head. "It is no woman's job. I'll send men after him at dawn."

"Take your hands off me! I refuse to sit around and do nothing like you all did when he went looking for me in Constantinople," Gigi raged. "I swear I'm going to Ravenna, right now, whether you help me or not, whether you think I can or not."

Athaulf stared hard at her for several moments, then shrugged and let her go. "So be it. I'll see you have a fast horse and provisions. Wear the clothes you'll need and leave the rest behind. Take the weapons I gave Magnus, and may God give you strength, because you will surely have need of them before this is over." He paused and looked even more closely at her. "Never allow Honorius to take you. It will go far better for both of you if you take your own life instead, for he will not kill you outright, but will torture you in each other's presence, you may be sure, so that your agonies and his delight are compounded."

Gigi bowed her head, horrified by his words, knowing they were true. "Please send Placidia to me while I get ready. I want to see her before I leave."

Athaulf nodded and Gigi raced to her tent. She threw on her warmest clothes, pulling on her heavy boots just as Placidia rushed in.

"Gigi!"

In tears, they hugged for a long moment. Finally, Gigi pulled away and looked at her friend. "Placidia, I have to go."

"Gigi, dearest Gigi," she cried. "You are so strong—so unafraid—I know you will save Magnus! Meet us at the villa as soon as . . . I pray God . . . I pray He grants you success."

Gigi kissed Placidia's brow, then slung her flute and short blade over her head, and grabbed Magnus's sword and dagger. She could hear the horse moving about outside and hurried from the tent.

Athaulf held the steed, and Gigi slipped Magnus's weapons into their straps, then jumped into the saddle. Placidia followed her out, looking stricken. Gigi's eyes welled, but she blinked her tears away, fighting for control.

"Gigi, your saddlebags are full of provisions. You must go by way of the Via Appia," Athaulf said, "then the Via Flaminia."

"I'm going to follow Magnus, wherever they're headed."

"And I'm telling you this is the route they'll take. There will be markers along the way, so you'll know."

She listened impatiently as Athaulf gave more travel advice, then handed her a pouch of coins. As soon as he let go of the bridle, she blew a kiss to Placidia and turned her horse, urging it toward the edge of camp and the road north.

One obstacle remained before she could pick up speed: a steep, boulder-strewn rise. Gigi allowed her mount to find his way up, knowing a clear path lay just over the crest. Once there, she'd be able to dig in her heels. For the moment, however, she had to keep herself from slipping over his rump. *Damn*, she thought, *what I wouldn't give for a pair of stirrups.*

A flash came out of nowhere, a bolt of fire, blinding her and causing the horse to lurch, hurtling her into the air. She hit the ground hard, the jolt making her vision blur, making it impossible to breathe.

Trying in vain to roll over and get her bearings, her limbs barely responded. She heard a familiar cackle, then looked around to see Randegund pick up the torch she'd flung. She hovered over Gigi with a sneer.

Gigi still couldn't move, stunned, certain she was about to die.

"I'll not have her polluted blood on my hands," Randegund whispered to herself, kneading her chest. "No, but I will take her blessed protection away from her, something her despicable flesh is not worthy to wear."

The world spun crazily. Gigi felt helpless as Randegund wrenched off her Roman ring, gathered her skirts, and then ran, her gleeful cackles echoing off the boulders. Gigi squeezed her eyes shut, then opened them, fighting vertigo. She caught torchlight flickering in the distance, but then it winked out, Randegund gone.

Head swimming, Gigi struggled to her knees and tried to make sense of her immediate surroundings. It was so dark. The horse snorted close by, waiting for its rider.

"Good boy," Gigi mumbled, and put a hand on a rock, forcing herself to her feet, gulping oxygen into her lungs. Staggering, she made her way to the horse and clutched his reins, then slowly, painfully, climbed onto a boulder and pulled herself into the saddle.

"Good boy," she repeated, grasping, entwining her fingers in his mane. Leaning forward, she rested her head on his neck, and then thudded her heels against his sides. "Now, find Magnus." Nothing. She gathered her willpower and tried again, but the beast only flinched, unsure of what she wanted.

What am I going to do? she wondered. The desperate situation both she and Magnus were in, the sheer odds against her success, threatened to crush her spirit. She looked down at her empty ring finger, her fear of losing Magnus made all the worse by Randegund's evil deed.

If I could only . . . if . . .

No! Her resolve, her inner strength surged back, and she summoned every ounce of her courage. *Forget the ring! Forget the witch! You can do this, Gigi!*

Save your husband!

She gathered the reins in one hand, sat up, and whipped the leather straps across the horse's haunches with as much violence as she could muster.

"Yah! Move it!" she shouted, and her chest seized, fighting for every breath. The beast leapt forward, nearly unseating her again, but she held on and dug in her heels a third time.

Together, they sped into the night, north to find Magnus, north to Ravenna.

*

The wind bore Randegund up the rocky slope, blowing at her back, hurling her forward.

Her left arm burned, throbbed with pain, and she blamed Magnus's damnable ring for this new agony. She looked at her aching hand, wishing she could cast the ring to the winds, but not yet, not yet. Soon, she thought, for dawn was near, and then she would be rid of this terrible burden.

She stared out. The clouds were gray, low, but lifting from the horizon, the barest slash of color in the sky, as red as the hideous ring.

Final, tortuous steps. Randegund forced her leaden legs to move on. The summit lay just before her.

Suddenly, her chest exploded with crushing pain and she lost her footing, dropping to her knees. Gasping for air, she sensed Nemesis had attacked, lashing out and passing through her, in search of Victoria. She clutched the ring in her trembling fist, intending to fling it with a renewal of her old curse, but instead her eyes closed and she felt nearly paralyzed by the bone-shattering agony in her breast.

Then, abruptly, a vision seized her and Randegund saw an image of Magnus and Gigi kneeling over a prostrate Honorius. Magnus held something vile in his hand, something dark and phallic, yet a symbol of the Old Ones who worshiped fertility— surely a sign. She knew then he had it in his power to kill the emperor, the epitome of all-evil, Rome incarnate, yet Magnus appeared to hesitate.

No, no! With heart-stopping clarity, she realized this was the moment she had always foreseen, when Magnus could turn the world on its end, when he would become the destroyer of Rome and then live to regret what he had done, for in killing Honorius, he would also bring about his own destruction and that of . . .

New images surged into her thoughts: of Honorius crying out

for his guards just before he died; then the bitch wife, Gigiperrin, dying horribly before Magnus's eyes, her body hacked to pieces by the axes of the imperial guards, just after they rushed through the door; and finally Magnus's fitting end: castration first, and then death by beheading.

With a last burst of strength, Randegund flung the ring into the air, intending to honor Nemesis by laying another curse on Magnus, to seal his fate and make sure he killed Honorius—but she found her mouth would not open, and she could not form the needed words.

"Ahhhh!" she managed to cry as the ring spun skyward and flamed, caught in the sun's first rays. Then, with a final gasp, she tried to speak, but the only word that escaped was, "Onward."

Birth. Love. Loss. Hatred. Revenge. Devastation. Randegund saw the long coil of her life twisting through time. And she knew Nemesis and Victoria and all the gods would vie with each other for thousands of years, time rolling ever onward. Yet once and a day, time would come 'round, like a viper striking its own tail, and the gods would rest for the briefest moment, before starting anew.

With her last breath, Randegund fell and her agony ceased: Nemesis had released her.

Stillness now, a last glimpse of pale pink sky, and then she was swallowed whole by a darkness like she never saw, the deepest, blackest night.

PART THREE

Chapter 17

Sunset was fast approaching, the full moon rising in the east. From a hill overlooking a valley already bathed in shadows, Gigi scanned the lowlands, watching the Roman soldiers who held Magnus. She wished she had the strength in numbers to sweep down into their camp and rescue him. But that was only a fantasy. She knew, until they reached Ravenna, all she could do was follow them, watch, and wait.

Gigi blew on her hands to ward off the cold. Standing in a copse of trees, she pulled close the heavy wolf-skin cloak draped over her shoulders. She didn't dare light a fire for warmth, as the soldiers had done, but the fur kept her warm enough.

The temperature had fallen drastically after she left the Visigoth camp, and snowdrifts were a foot deep by the end of the first day. Now, three days later, the wind had stopped howling, but the snow was two feet deep, and her horse had to move slowly, choosing his footing with care. At first, the frigid weather had worried her, but she soon realized the snow provided two huge benefits; it was far better than soaking rain, and it made a simple task out of tracking her husband and his abductors. She'd even begun to develop a sense of how fresh the tracks were, if she was getting too close, or perhaps lagging too far behind.

The Roman camp was a long way off, but she could smell the wood smoke and whatever sort of gruel they had boiling in their pot. Her stomach rumbled with hunger and she turned away, harshly reminding herself the dried meats and grains Athaulf had provided were nourishment enough.

Keeping an eye on the distant blaze, she made both a blind and a makeshift bed by cutting tender bows off nearby trees and propping the longer ones against a low-lying branch, piling the smaller ones on the ground beneath. When this was done, she brought her horse from its hiding spot on the far side of the hill, tying him beneath the shelter of tree limbs as well. Then she fixed her cold camp as best she could, grabbing a piece of mutton jerky from her pack before settling down.

Sitting with her back against a tree trunk, Gigi faced the Roman camp, its men and horses black shapes against the flames on this moonlit night. She chewed thoughtfully, watching over Magnus the only way she could, wondering if he sensed her thoughts, her devotion, hoping he did.

*

The horse snorted and shook his head, waking Gigi. It was past dawn, and the sky was overcast, the clouds sickly yellow, threatening. She stood and peered at the area where the Romans' campfire had been, seeing only a dark spot on the snow. Moving carefully, stiff with cold, Gigi saddled her horse, mounted, and approached the site with caution.

The imprint of their stay was obvious from the churned-up, dirty slush and the cold remnants of last night's fire. Gigi dismounted and shoved at the bits of charred wood with the toe of her boot, then knelt and stretched out her hands. Even the meager warmth still emanating from the very center was more heat than she'd enjoyed in days, and she took a moment to relish the sensation and consider her situation.

This was her fifth morning on the road. Athaulf warned it could take ten days or more to get to Ravenna. Her provisions were holding out for now, and she still had all of the silver coins he'd given her to purchase more along the way, but she knew she would have to find a farmhouse today and get fodder for the horse, and maybe some hot porridge for herself.

Rising, she scanned the ground, noticed a glint in the snow near the base of a tree, and went to investigate. Somebody had stepped off to pee—the snow told her that much—but the glint came from something else, something just to the side.

Gigi's breath caught as she picked up Magnus's locket, the one with her hair. She knew he'd left it for her to find. He knew she was coming for him. He knew he wasn't alone.

She held the precious object to her breast, then kissed it and put it around her neck. He had faith in her, in her courage, in her love for him.

I'm coming! You're not alone!

The words struck her deeply and she remembered what he'd said long ago, when she was a slave and he was watching over her, protecting her. *You're not alone!*

She was determined to honor those words as he'd honored them—by doing whatever it took to see him safe and free of Honorius's relentless evil.

Gigi turned and ran back to her horse.

She wouldn't let him down.

*

At dusk on the tenth day since setting out, Gigi finally arrived on the outskirts of Ravenna. The southern gate, the Porta Nuova, loomed above her, opening onto the main road through town, the Via di Roma. Peasants, merchants, horses, and livestock all pushed toward the gate, anxious to get inside Ravenna's walls before dark. The crowd was bundled up against the cold, but the weather didn't seem as bad here, not compared to the snowy countryside. The snow had either melted, or perhaps never fallen this far north; the skies were clear, the air crisp.

Keeping her head low and well inside her cloak, she moved past the guards at the gate, relieved no one paid her any attention.

my chores. He promised he would wait for me, and, er, I have bathed as he asked."

"He didn't speak of it to me," the guard countered. "Besides, he has received another, uh, guest, and I'm sure he does not want to be bothered. Be gone."

Pouting, Gigi looked up at the man and blinked several times. "It was an order, and I would not care to ignore such a direct request. If he doesn't want to see me anymore, I'm sure he'll say so, but please, I don't think either one of us should presume to know his mind."

He hesitated, looking uncertain and uneasy, and Gigi's thoughts veered to what might be happening behind those doors.

"Go on then," the guard huffed, letting her pass. "Be it on your head alone if he takes it ill!"

Gigi headed for the second set of doors, where a pair of bored-looking sentries stood. Through the walls, she could hear yelling and laughter and recognized Honorius's voice at once. Her arms started to shake, but she put her chin up and forced her gaze down.

"At the emperor's request," she said, holding up the tray.

To her relief, the men stood aside and let her in, and the doors shut behind her. Honorius was across the room, pacing, ranting, paying no attention to her, and Magnus was on his knees before the emperor, bare-chested and bloody, head bowed, arms bound behind his back.

Gigi gulped back a cry and crouched behind the large bed. She put the tray on the floor, then pulled off the *palla* and drew out her dagger and Magnus's short blade. Just as she was about to rise, she heard footsteps approaching from the opposite side, and something heavy landed on the bed. The footsteps receded, and Gigi rose slightly, to see what was going on.

Honorius's clothing was in a heap on the bed and he was naked, standing before Magnus with a barb-tipped leather whip in his hand.

Horrified, Gigi looked at Magnus and suddenly realized he wasn't kneeling on purpose, and it wasn't just a bloodied nose he'd suffered, but much, much worse. There were open, bleeding cuts across his chest, shoulders, and arms, and he was tied against a column to keep him upright. She cried out. Magnus was unconscious!

Honorius spun around and Gigi saw expressions of fury, then shock, and finally delight pour over his face as he moved toward her.

Then she saw the bastard's erection.

Enraged, ready to kill, she leapt to her feet, holding both blades in front of her. *"You sonofabitch,"* she said in English, *"you're going to die for this!"*

She stepped away from the bed, making sure of her surroundings, always keeping him before her, as Athaulf's boys had taught her.

"Gigiperrin," Honorius cooed, swinging the whip back and forth, his cock whipping side to side as well, "we should have known you'd come running to save your lover, although we're afraid there'll not be much of him left when we are done. For all we know, he's dead already."

Suddenly terrified, Gigi glanced at Magnus again. Was he breathing? She couldn't tell.

As if in response, he moaned just as Honorius lunged, snapping the whip at her head, but she leapt away just in time. She thrust one of her blades toward him, but missed by several inches and he laughed at her efforts. She pivoted and faced him again, heart pounding. *Get closer next time,* she told herself. *Draw him in.* She swallowed hard, quelling her instinct to run.

Honorius grinned. "So, the whore-slave has yet to learn humility, but we shall see what we can do about that."

With a flick of his wrist, he sent the tip of the whip flying at her again and Gigi heard herself scream as she raised her arm defensively, then scream again as pain ripped through her senses. Not only had the thing cut her forearm, she was surprised to see the thin leather braid had wrapped around her elbow. Furious, she jerked the whip as hard as she could and glanced up when she heard Honorius cry out.

"Magnus," she whispered up to him, "let go and fall backward on three, do you understand? One, two . . . three."

There was a slight hesitation, but then he let go, and she could see him falling, dropping, and suddenly the sheet went taut and nearly jerked her off her feet. Catching her breath, she couldn't help but grin as Magnus swung easily on the other end of the line, looking pleased and bewildered. Then, gradually, Gigi let the sheet play through her hands until Magnus's feet touched the ground.

She untied him, pulled the cloak over his head, and tossed the *palla* over her shoulders, then wadded up the sheeting and hid it behind a bush. With one shoulder propping him up, Gigi and Magnus made their way through the grounds, heading for the garden, and hopefully, the horse would still be tied there, waiting to take them out of town.

Whenever she saw guards, Gigi hid with Magnus until they passed. Twice she had nowhere to hide and was forced to pull Magnus against her in an embrace, so the guards would only see the cloak. Both times, they started to ask questions, but as soon as she giggled and manipulated Magnus's hips, they backed off quickly, full of apologies to the emperor.

Exhausted and worried Honorius would sound the alarm at any minute, Gigi and Magnus moved as fast as possible, heading for Venus's garden—and freedom.

Chapter 18

The moon hid behind silver-edged clouds. Using her shoulder, Gigi supported Magnus, guiding him down the path into the depths of the garden. She was terrified by the crunch of gravel beneath their feet, the sound magnified by the night and her fear. Stumbling on, she was relieved when the gravel finally gave way to dirt and weeds. Magnus felt so heavy, and he was groaning more often, but this only made her more determined to reach the tumbledown wall and her horse.

We're almost there, she thought, willing herself on. *We're almost there.*

She had been aware for some time of dampness spreading across her shoulder. This was bad. He was bleeding too much!

Gigi could hardly see in the gloom, the path overgrown and so dark, the naked vines pulling at them, raking like claws. Magnus's steps were unsteady, like he was drunk, and she adjusted her gait, bracing herself to counteract his ever-increasing wobbliness. But just when Gigi feared their legs would give out, the vines disappeared, and they emerged into the clearing.

She could barely see the statue of Venus guarding the frozen pool, and to her relief, she heard her horse's gentle snorts. *Good. No one has taken him.*

"Magnus," she whispered, halting by the little bench, "we're in the garden. We're almost safe. I have a horse waiting on the other side of the wall."

He managed a slight groan and whispered, "I don't think . . . I can't go on. Save yourself."

"No," she whispered back. "We're staying together no matter what."

The moon slid from behind the clouds, and the luminous statue glowed at the center of her columned temple and icy pool.

mounted his horse. "Yah!" he shouted, welcoming the surge of muscle beneath him.

Despite the cold night air, the hard ride, Sarus was suddenly drawn back to a cozy image, a snatch of a dream, which enveloped him in a palpable feeling of warm expectation. Images and sensations flitted through his mind: peering down at the sandy floor of the arena, the continual roar of the crowd, a rush of deep satisfaction, and then the dream came back full-blown, and he saw the rotting corpse of that bastard Alaric, murderer of his family, being torn apart by jackals. Sarus smiled, recapturing his exultation as he sat by Honorius's side in the royal enclosure. Laughing uproariously together, they beheld the spectacle of Alaric's final defilement.

But . . . was the dream a portend? Would it become reality?

He frowned. Honorius was a fool for not letting him question Magnus first, for Sarus knew he could get the location of Alaric's tomb out of the bastard's traitorous mouth. Honorius had not the talent for subtle torture, and now he had let Magnus escape.

Then Sarus chewed on another thought: the female slave who aided Magnus must be none other than that bitch of a flute player in disguise. Of course! Who else would have known he'd been brought here?

Perhaps she also knew where Alaric's corpse had been buried. Torturing her in front of Magnus's eyes would no doubt loosen his tongue, for he was besotted with her, and if he didn't reveal the location, she certainly would.

Riding on, Sarus was glad he had not divulged the true details of his plan to Sergeric. For all his failings, his younger brother was loyal to his people and would never reveal the location of a Visigoth king's tomb. In fact, even Honorius had not guessed the real purpose of Sarus's plan, so engrossed was he by his own vulgar desires.

But it was now clearer how things might play out, with a little luck. Yesterday, Sarus had received word the new king, Athaulf— *may he be cursed!*—was leading his people north, to winter in the shelter of the Sabine Hills, near Hadrian's Villa.

Sarus was certain Magnus and Gigi would be heading there as well. Indeed, he thought, tonight they would try to leave by Ravenna's southern gates.

He nudged his mount to the left, southward, then motioned for his men, fifty strong, to follow.

*

Gigi heard the distant drumming of hooves. She glanced over her shoulder, listening, trying to ignore her thudding heart.

Horses were coming their way, they were coming!

She didn't know what to do. Dozens of horsemen with torches burst into sight at the far side of the square and Gigi was forced to make a desperate decision. There was no hope of evading them, no hope of outrunning them.

There was only one option, one choice left.

"Magnus," she whispered as she reined in, "Magnus, we need to get off now."

She slid down, helped him dismount, and then slapped the horse's rump, sending it trotting back toward the moonlit square.

A moment. It was all she had. Turning, Gigi set off through the shadows, helping Magnus along, moving as fast as she could go.

*

Sarus saw the riderless horse. Was this a diversion? Where were they? He reined in and looked around, his men already fanning out in all directions, searching, shouting, sensing blood.

At first he saw nothing, but then he caught sight of two dim shapes moving beneath the plane trees.

He turned his horse's head and shouted, "There they are!"

*

Just as they reached the door of the baptistery, Gigi heard someone shouting. She propped Magnus against the wall and started pounding on the door, working the latch, yelling, "Help! Please, let me in. Hurry! I am a woman in need! Help me!"

Gigi glanced over her shoulder, then pulled out Magnus's sword, thrusting it into his hands. His eyes seemed to focus and he stood straighter, gripping his weapon, ready to challenge the horsemen bearing down on them. Gigi continued pounding the door. "Please, let me in! Hurry, hurry! Please, hurry!"

The door opened, and Gigi barely had time to react, catching herself from falling in just as the watchman gaped at what was happening over her shoulder.

"Magnus!" she shouted, pushing the man away before he could close the door on them.

To her relief, Magnus followed her inside, then fell against the door, closing it. She took his hand and pulled him up the steps to the pulpit.

"Block the door!" Gigi shouted to the watchman, but the man shook his head and backed away.

Only seconds remained. This was it. The moment when . . .

"Magnus, hold on to me," Gigi said, then yanked her flute from its leather sling.

If this doesn't work . . .

Magnus grabbed her, nearly knocking her into the font, but she managed to stay upright. She put the flute to her trembling lips, thinking of home, of that moment years ago when she played "The Minute Waltz," when she'd heard another flutist from far off, their music meshing note for note, when her life changed forever.

Her hands shook, and she cursed herself—jelly fingers! It took precious moments before she willed a semblance of composure and started to play. A few off-key notes issued from the flute, and she summoned all of her willpower to blow true.

Music filled the room, clear and lively, and she played on,

gaining confidence, hoping, hoping, the air whirling with color. She heard an answering call and paused briefly to hear the faint sound of another flute, then began again with relish.

Magnus held her, his eyes wide with astonishment. Her gaze darted toward the watchman, who had fallen to his knees, then down at the door where a group of Roman soldiers stood, mouths open, staring up at them.

As the air around her twinkled, the other flutist matched her note for note, the melodies merging, beautiful, electrifying. Suddenly, Gigi saw the other player, a man in a garish purple toga, his fingers flashing gold, his flute silver. In the next instant, he vanished and she heard a solitary cry pierce the air.

Play! Play! She squeezed her eyes shut, frantically played. But she felt nothing like before, no roaring, no floor giving way.

Play harder! The notes were shrill, like a shriek or an agonizing wail, a pitiful prayer, and in desperation she played on and on.

Suddenly, Magnus let go and fell back against the pulpit. *No, no!*

Devastated, Gigi dropped her flute and grasped at him in fear, clutching him in farewell, weeping. She knew death was imminent—or worse, that they would face Honorius again, very, very soon.

She blinked away her tears and saw sunshine bathing Magnus in its glow, a last, beautiful moment of life in his arms.

"I love you, Magnus. I love you."

He opened his eyes, then glanced over her shoulder and frowned, clearly sensing something.

She cringed and listened for the soldiers' footsteps, then caught her breath, hearing instead the unmistakable sounds of . . . *traffic?*

Gigi stared at Magnus. *Could it possibly be?* Turning toward the entrance, she saw the kiosk and modern doorway, sunlight streaming in through the open door.

"Oh, my God."

Hardly daring to believe, Gigi willed herself to accept the truth her senses were proclaiming—this was real!

"I, I think we made it," she stammered. A wave of relief swept over her, and she started to help Magnus to his feet, but to her horror, his skin felt even colder than before, and his teeth were chattering again.

The sword dropped from Magnus's hand, clattering on the floor, and he grimaced, then groaned and leaned against her. She had to get him help quickly. Using what little strength she had left, she supported him and they stumbled from the building.

As they entered the day-lit garden, time seemed to flesh out, capturing and holding them in the present, her present. Gigi took one deep breath after another, reveling in the modern scents of café food and vehicle exhaust, hearing the wonderful cacophony of mopeds and horns honking and rock music blasting from a car stereo. *Home*, her mind soared. *Home!*

A group of women tourists surged forward, waving cameras and chattering in English. They stopped short when they saw Gigi and Magnus.

"Brilliant!" one exclaimed, her British accent thick. "Are we in time for a reenactment?"

The ladies began talking all at once and it took a long moment for Gigi to adjust to their spate of rapid-fire English.

Just as she was about to open her mouth, one of them stepped forward and spoke above the rest, "What in the world is she wearing beneath her shawl—burlap? If you ask me, neither of them looks very authentic, not like Horace. I want my picture taken with Horace." She looked down her nose at Magnus. "Dear Lord, is he drunk?"

"No, he's not drunk!" Gigi flared. "He's been injured and needs help. Do any of you have a cell phone?"

Eyebrows shot up all around, but before the ladies could react further, Magnus lost his footing and tumbled down. Crying out, Gigi fell to her knees beside him, then noticed her hands were covered in fresh blood. Several of the women screamed, drawing passersby from every direction.

"Call 911!" Gigi yelled. Holding Magnus, she heard frantic conversations in Italian, French, Japanese, and then English again, with someone shouting above the others, "Call 311—it's 311 in Italy!"

A white-haired woman suddenly pushed through the crowd and knelt beside Gigi. "*Signorina*, I am a physician," she said in accented English. "I have called the hospital and an ambulance is on the way." She touched Magnus's throat, feeling for a pulse, then lifted an eyelid to examine his pupil. Magnus blinked, which reassured Gigi he was still alive.

"Did he fall? Can he move his legs?" the doctor asked.

Gigi nodded. "He was cut and, and poisoned . . . given belladonna . . . and something to make him bleed."

The woman gaped at her, then shook her head and started checking his bandages. Sirens blared, police vans and an ambulance arrived, and the crowd was moved back.

"*Signorina, andatevene!*" an emergency worker said, pushing Gigi aside as they wheeled in a gurney.

The physician spoke quietly to them, and Gigi heaved a sigh. *He's going to live, he's okay,* she kept telling herself as she watched them set up an IV in Magnus's arm. *He's safe now, he's going to make it.*

She followed Magnus to the ambulance and got inside, forgetting to thank the doctor who had done so much for him. One of the English women ran up and shoved the flute and sword at her. "Are these yours? I found them—"

Sirens started again, and Gigi mouthed "thank you" and took their things, just as the medics closed the doors.

She reached for Magnus's hand. It felt warmer, and she heard him draw breath, a deep sigh. Suddenly, her tensions eased and she rested her head on his chest, exhausted, relieved. They were finally beyond Honorius's reach, somewhere he could never threaten them again. Gigi smiled, the bastard was dead, long dead, and they were here, alive.

She listened to Magnus's beating heart and realized all she had been through had a purpose, now that she'd brought him to her world, to safety—and freedom.

"I love you, Magnus. You're going to live. You'll be fine," she whispered to him, not expecting a response.

He squeezed her hand.

Chapter 19

Winter, A.D. 411, Hadrian's Villa

At Hadrian's Villa, in the craggy hills east of Rome, Placidia stood wrapped in a heavy cloak. At long last, she felt a measure of contentment. "It eases my heart to see our people well housed and well fed, if only for a brief while."

Elpidia shivered. "I would like it even better if you would take yourself inside, for some warmth and a bit of food."

Placidia smiled. "I told Athaulf I would meet him here. We enjoy watching the sun set over the reflecting pool. Go on and get your meal. There are guards everywhere. I'll be all right—there, you see, he's already here!"

Placidia waved happily as her handsome husband strode toward her. His smile, the way his eyes danced when he looked at her, the way his athletic body moved, everything about him worked a spell on her, every time she saw him.

The sound of hooves interrupted her thoughts, but she was used to this. Although Athaulf's kingship was still new and the demands on him constant, he was a natural leader, who took great pride in caring for his people. She watched as a small group of horsemen clambered to a stop. As they dismounted, Placidia saw a thin girl near her own age, sitting behind one of the riders. When Athaulf approached and the girl was helped down, she dropped to her knees. He raised her up, and together they spoke in hushed tones.

More news from afar, Placidia thought, curious as to the stranger's identity.

"Whoever she is, it's clear she hasn't brought good news," Elpidia grumbled, as she turned to leave. "Another of Honorius's victims having to beg for food, I shouldn't wonder."

Placidia didn't comment as she watched Athaulf and the girl break away from the horsemen and walk toward her. She was blond and tall, with the look of the *Germani* people, yet there was something else Placidia couldn't put her finger on, something familiar . . . her clothes!

Placidia rushed forward and took the girl by the shoulders, immediately noticing the slave collar and nasty brand on her forehead. "You are wearing Gigi's clothing!" she exclaimed. "Who are you? What happened to Gigi?"

Once again, the girl sank to her knees, this time a great sob tearing from her chest. "Vana. I am Vana. I am . . . I was a slave at the palace and knew Gigi well. I saw her come in one night, many days ago. She gave me her clothes and some coin. She told me I was free, to escape while I could, and bade me find you here. I swear it!"

Placidia fought panic, sank to her knees, and wrapped her arms around Vana's shoulders. "You are safe now, safe with us," she said, managing to control her voice. "You are free. But tell me, do you know anything more about Gigi, or her husband, Magnus? We hope they may find their way here, too, very soon. We look for them daily."

Vana's shoulders shook as her sobbing increased. "She . . . was going to find Honorius that night. I did not know why, although now I know it was to save Magnus. I left the palace kitchen, as Gigi ordered. I ran and, thank God, I escaped Ravenna."

Trembling, Placidia rose and tried to pull Vana to her feet. "Where are Gigi and Magnus?" she asked again, but the girl's agony redoubled, robbing her of speech.

Placidia felt a chill and looked at Athaulf, reading the dread in his eyes. As one, they again knelt beside Vana.

"Tell us," Athaulf coaxed, "tell us what you know."

"There was a great commotion the following morning. I was already in the countryside, but even there everyone spoke of it. They said all Ravenna was celebrating, and Honorius was heaping great honors upon a general . . . one Sarus, because . . . he, he delivered Magnus and Gigi to the palace—"

"Oh, my God, no!" Sobs caught in Placidia's throat, tears welled in her eyes. "Are they, will they be executed? I must write to my brother—"

"No! It is said there was a chase, and this general cornered them in a shack. When they refused to come out, he," Vana covered her eyes, keening, hardly able to form the words, "he burnt it down around them, then delivered . . . God help us all . . . delivered the charred corpses to Honorius."

"No!" Placidia screamed. Sagging into Athaulf's arms, she sobbed. "No, no, no!" Dreadful words played and replayed in her mind as though screaming at her, mocking her: *Delivered the charred corpses, delivered the charred corpses . . .*

Then, another voice, her husband's anguished voice, quieted them, if only for a moment. Coming to her ears, as though from a great distance, she heard, "By God, Sarus will pay for this. I swear before God, he will not see another spring."

Time became meaningless for Placidia as horror dimmed the world around her, as grief engulfed her and dragged her into dark oblivion.

Chapter 20

Present Day, Ravenna, Italy

Hiding behind sunglasses and a dark wig, Gigi fortified herself with two Bloody Marys at a bar near the hospital, where Magnus was recovering. So far, no one knew she was back except her manager, Jack, and her parents, who were en route from Seattle.

Clutching her new flute case, she purchased her ticket to the Mausoleum of Galla Placidia. Her flute was examined as she passed through security, but then they waved her on. With a deep breath, she hurried after the guide and other tourists toward the entrance of the rather plain-looking brick structure.

"As you will see," the tour guide said as he entered, his voice echoing, "the interior is breathtaking, perhaps the most beautiful in the world, even more so than Ravenna's other golden mosaics, which were said to inspire such literary luminaries as Dante and Yeats. In fact, this ceiling was the inspiration for Cole Porter's beautiful song, "Night and Day." The mausoleum was originally part of a much larger structure, the Church of the Holy Cross, which fell into ruin long ago. What remains is called a mausoleum, but historians believe it was originally the oratory of the Holy Cross. It is said to contain the most perfectly preserved mosaic ceiling from the ancient world, hence our designation as a UNESCO World Heritage Site."

Removing her sunglasses, Gigi stepped over the threshold and looked up, captivated by the gorgeous gold and blue mosaics of stars and angels. Nothing could have prepared her for the impact of seeing this place in person. She thought back, remembering another ceiling depicting the night sky, and the lovely, dark-haired young woman standing beneath it, so vibrant and alive.

Placidia. Tears threatened, and Gigi could feel her presence still, remembering the warmth of her smile, her brave heart. *What happened to you?* she wondered. *Did you grow old with Athaulf, sharing your love for years? Did you have children?*

Gigi had no idea—yet. And what of the others? Verica? Little Berga and the boys? With a tremor of expectation, she willed her thoughts back through time, hoping somehow she had made a difference for them as well.

She'd been holed up with Magnus in his hospital room since their arrival, but once he was out of danger—and at his urging—she'd decided to give herself this gift of time and knowledge.

A shuffling of feet and fading conversation brought Gigi around, and she realized the tour group was moving away from her. She started after them, straining to hear the guide.

"Look at the light, how the translucent mica in the windows casts an amber glow on the room," he was saying. "Wonderful, isn't it? And now, let us examine some of the mausoleum's other treasures, our three marble sarcophagi, precious relics of ancient Rome! You will notice they are plain, bearing no insignia except *Alpha Christus Omega*, signifying 'Christ is the Beginning and the End.' Scholars believe the central sarcophagus contained the remains of Galla Placidia."

Contained? Gigi wondered. *She isn't here?* Waving her hand to get the guide's attention, she called out, "Excuse me, where is she?"

"Unfortunately," the tour guide replied, "her body was destroyed by fire."

Stunned, Gigi stared at him.

The guide nodded soberly. "Yes, it was a horrible loss. When the tomb was first opened in the sixteenth century, the remains were found seated upright on a chair of cypress, dressed in royal robes and holding the imperial regalia. Unfortunately, the body was accidentally burned by some hooligans in 1573, when they introduced lighted tapers into the chinks of the tomb to see what lay inside. And now, ladies and gentlemen, if you would follow me."

Poor Placidia, how awful! Gigi barely heard the guide's next words, didn't care if she seemed rude as she waved again. "When did she die?"

He turned and smiled patiently at her. "She died of natural causes in the Year of Our Lord 450, on the twenty-seventh of November, to be exact. And now, if you would please join me over here."

She died in 450? Gigi felt exultant. *Placidia lived a long life!*

She lingered for a moment by the tomb. Gently running her hand over the cool marble, she remembered the last, hurried hug they shared. She wished she'd had the foresight to realize it would be their final goodbye.

Willing away the lump in her throat, she removed her flute. "Farewell, my dearest friend." Her voice caught and she stood there for a long moment, fighting tears, before whispering, "I will never forget you."

Gigi placed the flute to her lips. Fingers trembling, she blew the first notes low and faint, then sought to center herself, searching for her core of strength, needing to do this right.

Her heart surged with the deep love of one friend for another, and the melody floated out, haunting, lovely, so right for this place, this moment—a tribute to a great lady.

"Night and Day."

Chapter 21

Present Day, Sivota, Greece

The first stars shone in the velvet-blue sky, and the sailboat bobbed lazily in the cove, anchored a few dozen yards off little Mikri Ammos beach. Gigi smiled at Magnus as he sat in the back corner of the deck, his head resting against the railing.

Shirtless and barefoot, he wore long, baggy shorts, sunglasses, and had a three-day growth of beard. Most of his scars would fade in time, thanks to skillful plastic surgery, but beneath his bandages, they were still red and painful looking, although he swore he felt fine.

Gigi flicked her cell phone shut and kissed him lightly, barely brushing her lips against his. "It's getting dark, handsome," she said in English. "You don't need the shades any more."

"I speaking not good English today," Magnus said, smiling. He pushed the sunglasses onto his forehead and switched back to Latin. "And you told me I look good with them on. I was just aiming to please."

"I've made a decision," Gigi said in Latin, sitting next to him. "I want to sponsor music schools for kids in places where they'd have no access otherwise. Something to inspire them, give them dreams."

Magnus nodded. "That sounds wonderful, but what made you think of this?"

"Teaching Athaulf's children. I think about them all the time."

"As do I, but we are here now and can do no more for them." He kissed her hand. "So, your parents will arrive when?"

"Noon tomorrow—I can hardly wait! They're in London right now, waiting for a flight to Athens. I'm glad we decided to get out of Ravenna and meet them here. Jack was sure the *paparazzi* were on our trail and would've mobbed us if we'd stayed. None of us could have taken that."

Magnus pulled her close and Gigi rested her head on his chest, listening to the rumble of his voice as he said, "And they flew through the skies from the far side of the Earth, taking only a day?"

"Indeed, in a *jet*."

Magnus groaned and shook his head. "It would be too unsettling, too unnatural to travel like that."

Gigi kissed his chin. "I used to fly all the time, and so will you, soon." She switched to English. *"It's no big deal."*

"No, it too big deal," he countered, then switched to Latin again. "I'll follow on horseback, if you don't mind. What have you told them about me?"

Shrugging, Gigi gazed out over the water toward the small, quiet beach, the lush dark hills surrounding it, and the very few twinkling lights. "Jack really freaked when I disappeared. He was sure I'd been kidnapped. I told him the truth, but I told my parents it was love at first sight, we ran off and eloped, and now we're back. I apologized about a million times, but I'm not sure my family will ever get over the shock . . . until they spend time with you, of course. Then they'll understand."

"You don't plan to tell them the truth?" Magnus asked, surprised. "I believed you. Why wouldn't they?"

Gigi thought about his question. "Because mysterious things, unbelievable things like that just don't seem to happen any more. My parents are lawyers. They rely on empirical evidence and science and think just about everything is figured out. I mean, take earthquakes, for instance. You used to say it was the gods causing it, but now we know it's *plate tectonics*—and . . . whatever."

"Are you implying the gods have nothing to do with your *plate tectonics*?"

Gigi opened her mouth to respond, then closed it again and smiled. "Point taken, but still, something big like traveling through time—they'll think I've completely lost my mind."

"They may already think it based on what you've told them so far, and in that case what have you got to lose?" Magnus grinned.

She whacked him playfully on the thigh. "Fine, I'll tell them. Maybe speaking fluent Latin will help convince them, otherwise I don't know."

He gently fingered a strand of her hair. "It *was* love at first sight, you know, for me. You cast a spell from the very first moment."

Gigi snuggled closer. "I recall being a little too terrified to think along those lines at that moment, but I knew I could trust you the minute we looked at each other."

Magnus kissed her deeply, and a delicious heat coursed through her body. Pulling away slightly, she studied his wonderful face, his beautiful, blue eyes, as deep as the sea, and so full of love—all for her.

"I have something for you," she said. "I'd forgotten about it until I was packing for the ferry."

His brow furrowed, and he looked slightly worried. "Something for me?"

Gigi smiled and fished in her pocket, pulling forth his locket of rock crystal and gold. "You left this for me to find. I want you to have it back," she whispered.

Magnus sat up slowly and took the locket, amazement written across his features. "It never occurred to me . . . I just threw it in the snow with a prayer to Victoria. I never thought I would see it again."

Gigi reached up and helped him fasten it around his neck, then kissed him. "Let's go below decks and celebrate its return," she murmured.

He gazed at her, a flicker of amusement pulling at the corners of his mouth. "Not just yet, my sweet," he said, putting his arms around her and leaning back. "Not just yet. It's too beautiful out here, peaceful and . . . normal. Although it's unfortunate these," he waved his hand toward the path of contrails in the darkening sky, "*jets* mar the heavens as they pass. I don't like them at all."

He rested his head against the back of the seat. "Ah, here it is quiet. Aboard this boat, the world is as it should be. And you were right, that terrible day on the bluff at Rhegium—this Beneteau is truly a marvel, a wonderful sailing vessel. But I don't know how you do it. I really don't. The noise of your world, the rush—by the gods!—the speed of the ferry nearly stopped my heart. And those women on the beach today—baring their breasts in public—not that I minded looking—and men in Speedos, who've never held a weapon more lethal than a hot espresso, or a—what did you call it?—an iPhone?"

Gigi laughed at his odd tirade, wondering why he insisted on staying on deck, when she was so very ready to go below. "You're making fun of your kinsmen," she said. "And, by today's standards, Italian and Greek men are plenty virile, believe me."

"What about Jack?" Magnus went on. "I swear I knew him. He used to work as the master masseuse in the steambaths in Constantinople."

She laughed. "He's a good businessman and a good friend. He's had to pull plenty of favors since we got back, to smooth things over with the police, and then get you some identity papers, not to mention keeping the world in the dark, all without doubting my story. I'm sure he thought I was crazy, but he asked a lot of questions and eventually seemed to accept my word. He was stunned to see the worn out shape my flute was in, especially the key pads, since it'd only been a day for him since I disappeared, and I always kept it in top condition. Then, when my old boyfriend Yves called to find out what was going on, Jack talked the poor guy in circles, so Yves still doesn't know. He's going to think I'm so horrible when he finds out I'm in love with you. That's not a conversation I'm looking forward to!"

"I could run him through with my sword," Magnus offered, nuzzling her neck.

"Don't make fun of this. Yves and I were close before I left. From his point of view, I disappeared without a trace or a word of explanation, everyone was terrified with worry, and then I show up the next day, head-over-heels in love, and utterly without a decent excuse."

"I know, but you will make Yves understand, somehow, although I wouldn't chance telling anyone else but your parents the truth," Magnus said. "As for Jack, I like him. He helped me with something before we left Ravenna, while you were out arranging for our passage to Greece."

"What?" She looked at him, curious. "You spent time alone with Jack? What'd he help you with?"

"We snuck out of the hospital and went for a stroll, at my request," Magnus replied evasively.

Sitting up, Gigi stared at him. "I can't believe they let you out."

"The healers would have none of it at first, but relented when I agreed to ride in a rolling chair. I thought it demeaning, but the thing proved useful, for I was spent long before we were done."

"You're a good liar. You acted like you'd never seen a wheelchair before, when we left the hospital."

He smiled. "Wandering around Ravenna was a terrifying experience, I can assure you, recognizing nothing, and trying not to show how traumatized I felt by everything I witnessed—it's truly a wonder, this world of yours, wonderful and terrible all at once. At any rate, Jack and I spoke for some time, or rather, I gestured, drew several diagrams, and generally felt like an idiot, but eventually I got my point across, and he agreed to my wishes."

"But . . . what wishes?"

Magnus glanced toward the heavens. "I find I don't much care for *traffic*, but that is beside the point," he said, kissing her forehead. "It has grown dark, and I am glad of it, for the world looks as it should now, with the Milky Way giving us the only light we need."

"What wishes?" Gigi asked again, dying of curiosity.

"I borrowed what I'd guess is a rather large sum of money—Jack's money—and I apologize for that," he shifted uncomfortably, then smiled and looked frankly at Gigi, "but it seemed unlikely anyone would give me credit, based solely on my good name. No one seems to remember Quintus Pontius Flavus Magnus. In fact, from what I can tell, the only Romans well remembered in this time are Gaius Julius Caesar and Marcus Antonius. I must say, you live in a rather ignorant world—"

"That's fine! But what wishes?" she repeated in exasperation.

He laughed. "Well, it turns out I have something for you, too. You see, I thought," he reached into his pocket and drew out a small, dark box, "I thought it might be nice to renew our vows when your parents get here. After all, you tell me it's been sixteen hundred years since the last time we said them."

A delicious chill of anticipation swept over her.

Opening the box, Magnus presented her with a very large ruby ring, encircled by sparkling diamonds. The ring beautifully reflected the radiance of the night sky.

"Will you marry me, Gigi? Again?"

"Oh, Magnus." She held out a tremulous left hand, her third finger empty, so empty, since her struggle with Randegund. "*Yes, yes, yes*, I will marry you all over again."

Magnus grinned and slipped it on her finger, then gazed at her. "I wanted to look for something like the old one, but apparently the museums are rather reluctant to sell Roman *artifacts*," he kissed her, "and I think if they knew my true identity, they'd have me under glass before I could say a word in protest. As it is, they're sure I've stolen the sword Athaulf gave me. Jack assured me he would take care of that mess, too. At any rate, he seemed pleased with my intentions and said you would approve."

"It is beautiful and you are amazing and I love you dearly," Gigi murmured, overwhelmed. She wrapped her arms around his neck and kissed him deeply. "Can we please go downstairs now? We haven't made love in hundreds of years, after all."

"Granted," he laughed, "but there is more. Jack has arranged for a ceremony on this beach at dusk tomorrow, and then a feast to follow, just your parents and us. We shall take our vows once more, beneath the starry sky."

Gigi looked at him in wonder, then up at the heavens. It was so perfect. How had he known?

"You see," Magnus whispered into her hair, "Jack took me somewhere else that day . . . to Placidia's mausoleum, to see her ceiling, her beautiful legacy to the world. I think Placidia, being so very smart and a Christian, stayed well away from the infernal Styx and made her way up to the sky, to find her Heaven. And so, tomorrow, when we are wed, I know she will be looking down at us from above, blessing us with her love—and with everlasting happiness."

Grand-père, too, Gigi thought, blinking back tears.

She gazed at Magnus, seeing destiny unfold in the depths of his wonderful eyes, at peace now and filled with happiness. The hurt she'd seen before was gone, as distant as the time they'd left behind.

"I will always love you," she whispered.

"And I, you," he took her face in his hands and kissed her, "my divine Gigiperrin."

Authors' Note

Galla Placidia could easily have been one of Shakespeare's tragic heroines, her life shadowed as it was by misfortune and bitter loss. Yet she stands out as a figure of great humanity, coming down through the ages as a woman of keen intelligence and emotional resilience: occasionally girlish and rebellious, at other times fiercely passionate, a brave companion, and loyal wife.

Her relationship with Honorius does seem to have been challenging; her "abduction" by Athaulf after the sack of Rome shocking, their eventual union wholly understandable, given her looming future as the intended bride of the much older Constantius.

Some sources state Placidia was engaged to be married to Stilicho and Serena's son, Eucherius, and we have deliberately ignored this for the sake of clarity in our work. Other contemporary historians—Hydatius, Marcellinus Comes, and Jordanes chief among them—record the barest details of the capture of Placidia by Athaulf during the sack, while giving various supposed marriage dates taking place after our date of A.D. 410; in other words, no one really knows what happened between them during and after the sack or when they actually consummated their relationship. For the purposes of our novel, we ask the reader to enjoy our literary license in this regard.

Additionally, two versions of the circumstances leading up to the sack of Rome were given by the historian Procopius of Caesaria, who wrote his history around A.D. 550. Again, for clarity's sake, we have chosen to ignore his convoluted tale of young Visigoth males infiltrating Roman households as purported slaves, to await the appointed day and then rush the guards of the Salarian Gate, allowing their Visigoth brethren entry into Rome. Instead, we've woven our story around Procopius's other version, which involved a Roman woman Proba, who had her domestics open the gates, although we've fictionalized this, seizing upon the darker side to a woman's nature and giving Proba a reason for collusion with Sergeric, our traitorous Visigoth.

And the reasons for Placidia's apparent complicity in Serena's death have long been the subject of debate by historians. While her execution in Rome's Coliseum is historically accurate, we believe our fictional solutions as to the "why" of Placidia's actions reflect her overall character, giving the reader a clearer sense of what might have been.

As for Honorius, we trust we've captured his true character as well. Various historians describe him as debauched, lazy, incompetent, and without morals. He did love his chickens and guinea fowl, and did have them baptized. He also married both sisters, Maria and Thermantia, who were said to have remained virgins.

There are suggestions in some historical accounts that King Alaric's burial in the Busentinus River is myth; however, there are many others who claim its veracity, and we have chosen to use their version of history. Like so many frustrated treasure hunters who have searched for the gravesite over the centuries, we find the account too delicious to ignore.

As with all historical fiction, our story is woven around major personalities and events, keeping as true to actual history as possible. To put a twist on an old saying—the rest, as they say, is fiction.

About the Authors

Two authors writing as one, Cary Morgan Frates and Deborah O'Neill Cordes, specialize in recreating pivotal moments in history, epic adventure and romance—with a time travel twist. This is the second novel in their Roman time travel series. They live with their families in the Pacific Northwest.

In the mood for more Crimson Romance? Check out *Immortal Love* by Carmen Ferreiro-Esteban at *CrimsonRomance.com*.

Made in the USA
Lexington, KY
10 April 2013